"There was always one area of our marriage where we didn't seem to have any problems. Far from it, in fact."

It was hard to believe he was smiling. Tara might be feeling weak-kneed and hot because looking at him made her ache for him in the most carnal way, but she still couldn't believe his arrogance. Just because he knew she was no more immune to the sexual chemistry between them than he was, he had no right to think he was playing some kind of trump card.

"Sex isn't a particularly sound reason on which to base a marriage," she said huffily, wishing she didn't sound like some priggish little virgin.

"I agree." He flashed a deeply bone-melting smile, a weapon clearly designed to elicit the most devastating response, and Tara clenched her thighs tightly together beneath her dress to stop them from shaking.

"But *great* sex—mind-blowing, knee-trembling, all night long, 'we don't need to sleep' sex—now that's another thing altogether. Wouldn't you agree?"

The day **MAGGIE COX** saw the film version of *Wuthering Heights,* with a beautiful Merle Oberon and a very handsome Laurence Olivier, was the day that she became hooked on romance. From that day onward she spent a lot of time dreaming up her own romances, secretly hoping that one day she might become published and get paid for doing what she loves most! Now that her dream is being realized, she wakes up every morning and counts her blessings. She is married to a gorgeous man, and is the mother of two wonderful sons. Her two other great passions in life—besides her family and reading/writing—are music and films.

THE MARRIAGE RENEWAL

MAGGIE COX

PREGNANCIES OF PASSION

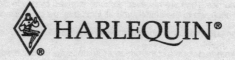

HARLEQUIN®

TORONTO • NEW YORK • LONDON
AMSTERDAM • PARIS • SYDNEY • HAMBURG
STOCKHOLM • ATHENS • TOKYO • MILAN • MADRID
PRAGUE • WARSAW • BUDAPEST • AUCKLAND

To my mum Norah,
who taught me to love books practically as soon as
I could talk and who always believed that one day
something really good would happen to me.

ISBN-13: 978-0-373-82039-9
ISBN-10:   0-373-82039-9

THE MARRIAGE RENEWAL

First North American Publication 2004.

Copyright © 2003 by Maggie Cox.

CHAPTER ONE

THE baby had distracted her. The beautiful, tow-haired, drooling baby, who had sat opposite her on his mother's lap, his gummy grin tying Tara's heart into knots and consigning all her well-intentioned plans to enjoy a carefree, happy day off to oblivion. *All because his name was Gabriel.* By the time she got off the train at Liverpool Street, tears had been welling like a dam about to burst, and she'd had to dig frantically through her purse for change for the ladies' toilet.

Staring at her reflection in the mirror, Tara dabbed at her streaked mascara, reapplied some blusher and sucked in several deep breaths to calm herself. *It was five years ago…five years.* So why hadn't she got over it? It had just been bad luck that the baby on the train had shared his name with another beautiful baby boy… She was tired, that was all. Long overdue for a holiday. Back at her aunt's antique shop, she had a drawer full of glossy brochures promising the destinations of a lifetime. Carefree, sun-kissed vistas that, if she ever got round to booking one, might remind her that she was just thirty years old, with a lot of life in front of her yet to have fun.

'The V&A,' she said out loud into the mirror, as if putting her resolve into words might give her the will and the desire to get there. She delved into her shoulder bag for a brush, quickly dragged it through her shoulder-length blonde hair, noted for the second time that day that her fringe was in dire need of a trim, then, straightening her shoulders, exited through a turnstile out into the familiar mêlée that was Liverpool Street Station. Twenty minutes later, revived by a take-away café latte, certain she was once more steering the ship, she headed determinedly down into the underground to board a tube and continue her journey to South Kensington.

Inside the museum it was almost unbearably close. Initially trying to shrug off the heat, Tara tried hard to concentrate on what she was looking at. Browsing some of the impressive historical-dress collection that spanned four centuries of European fashion—always her favourite place to start on a visit—she paused to remove her light denim jacket and comb her fingers through her hair. Her hand came away damp from her forehead. Then, worryingly, the room started to spin.

'Oh, my God.' Resting her head against one of the long glass cabinets, blinking at the blur of green and yellow that was some diminutive aristocrat's ballgown, Tara prayed hard for the spinning sensation to stop. If only she'd roused herself a few minutes earlier that morning then she wouldn't have had to fly out of the house to catch the early train—and she wouldn't have left the house on an empty stomach. Coupled with the shock of hearing a name that haunted her from the past, it meant that her equilibrium was now paying the price.

'Are you all right, dear?' An elderly lady with skin that resembled soft, crumpled parchment delicately laid her hand on Tara's shoulder. The faintest drift of lavender wafted beneath her nose. Touched by the kindness of a stranger, the younger woman opened her mouth to speak, to tell her concerned enquirer that she was perfectly fine; all she needed was to sit down for a couple of minutes then she'd be right as rain again—

but the words just wouldn't come. Inside her head Tara was frantically trying to assimilate the frightening sensation of hurtling towards the ground in a high-rise lift when suddenly her whole world tilted and she felt herself slide inelegantly to the floor.

'Tara…Tara, wake up. Can you hear me?'

She knew that voice. Knew it intimately. It was like the stroke of velvet whispering over her skin or the first seductive swallow of good French brandy on an icy cold day. All her nerve endings exploded into vibrancy. First the baby—now this…*his* voice when she hadn't heard it in over five long years… It had to be over-work, that was the only explanation.

Her heart was racing as her eyelids fluttered open. The high vaulted ceiling seemed miles away but that wasn't the sight that consumed her body and soul. It was the intense blue gaze beneath the ridiculously long sweep of thick blond lashes staring down at her that had her riveted. Not to mention the deep indentation in the centre of a hard, chiselled jaw and the perfectly defined cheekbones in a masculine face so captivating someone ought to paint it—just to prove for posterity that male beauty like this existed…

'Macsen.'

There was the briefest flinch in the side of his jaw in acknowledgement of his name but other than that Tara detected no discernible response. Disappointment, hurt, then confusion temporarily stalled her brain.

'Do you know this young woman?' It was the lady smelling of lavender. She was staring at the impressively built blond Adonis leaning over Tara as if she was going to demand some ID.

'Yes, I know her,' he replied in clipped tones tinged

with the slightest Scandinavian accent. 'She happens to be my wife.'

'Oh. Well, I don't think it was wise to let her wander around alone. She looks very peaky to me. Is she all right? Why don't you help her sit up and give her some of this water?' The woman helpfully produced a small bottle of mineral water from her voluminous bag.

'I'm all right. Really.' Struggling to a sitting position, Tara marvelled at her ability to be coherent when her heart was pushing against her ribcage as if it was about to burst. She'd fainted. That much was obvious. But where had Mac appeared from and what was he doing in the V&A? And of all the people who could have witnessed her embarrassing moment, why, oh, why did it have to be him? Apart from her elderly friend smelling of lavender, that was.

'Have you eaten?' Mac was already unscrewing the bottle of water, sliding his hand round the back of her head and guiding her lips towards it. Tara spluttered a little as the water filled her mouth and slid down her throat but it instantly made her feel better, more like herself.

'What do you mean, have I eaten?' Wiping her hand across her mouth, she was resigned to the fact that her lilac-coloured lipstick had probably been all but obliterated. Just because Mac's impossibly blue eyes were mesmerising her as they had always had the power to do, she couldn't really expect to look her best when she'd just passed out in front of him. But seeing him again was sweet agony to her beleaguered soul…

'She has a habit of forgetting to eat,' Mac confided aloud with what sounded suspiciously like resignation. 'This isn't the first time she's fainted.'

'She needs taking care of.' The woman accepted the

half-consumed bottle of water, screwed the top back on and returned it to her bag. 'Why don't you take her to the cafeteria and get her a sandwich?'

'Thank you. I was just about to do that very thing.' His tone deceptively charming, Mac bestowed one of his killer smiles on the older woman, which Tara knew just had to make her day, then brought his gaze slowly but deliberately back to her. As she swallowed hard, her heart skipped another beat.

'I don't want a sandwich.' Old resentment surfaced and, scrambling to her feet, Tara dusted down her long denim skirt, green eyes shooting defiant, angry little sparks that couldn't fail to tell him she didn't welcome his intervention—no matter how apparently kind. He was taking charge again...just as he had always done. How dared he? Had he forgotten they hadn't seen each other for five years? Did he think he could just walk back into her life and take up where he'd left off?

Of course he didn't. Her heart sank. She was being utterly foolish and stupid. If he'd wanted to take up where they'd left off he would have contacted her long before this. Long before she'd built an impenetrable fortress round her heart to stave off further hurt or disappointment.

'Well, take care, then...both of you.' With a doting smile—the kind reserved for beloved grandchildren—the elderly lady left them.

Tara ran her tongue round the seam of her lips then stole a furtive glance at Mac. He towered over her, tall, broad-shouldered, athletically lean and commanding in that impossibly arrogant way he had that made her feel very much 'the little woman,' no matter how emancipated she told herself she was. He was wearing his hair a little longer than she remembered but it was still straight, blond and unbelievably sexy. Tactile. Just begging for her to run her fingers through it...

A small trickle of perspiration slid down her back between her shoulder blades.

'What are you doing here?' Caught off-balance, she knew her voice lacked the strength it had normally. It made her stiffen her resolve to somehow stay immune to this man.

A beguiling dimple appeared at the corner of his mouth as he straightened the cuffs of his suit jacket—his very expensive suit jacket. 'Looking for you. What else?'

Mac watched her reluctantly eat her sandwich. She had that look on her face that said she was eating it under duress—not because it was good for her or because *he* thought she should. She was just as stubborn as he remembered, stubborn and...gorgeous. Simply ravishing in that fresh-faced English way, with her softly mussed blonde hair, milkmaid complexion and pretty green eyes like emeralds washed beneath a crystal-clear fountain.

He'd missed her. An odd little jump in the pit of his stomach attested to that. Suddenly unclear about his own intentions, he told himself to get a grip. All he had to do was tell her what he wanted and go. After which, he needed never set eyes on her again. Something in him baulked at that.

'My aunt had no business telling you where to find me,' Tara pouted, her plump lower lip sulky but undeniably appealing. 'Anyway, how did you know where to look?'

Stirring his coffee, Mac took a careful sip before

replying. 'You always used to come here first, remember? You loved looking at the clothes.'

She did. And more often than not she'd dragged Mac round with her, promising she'd go to one of his boring business dinners with him if he'd just humour her in this, her favourite pastime.

Another bite of sandwich found its way to her mouth. The tuna and mayonnaise filling could have been wallpaper paste for all she knew. Her tastebuds had ceased to function while her stomach was mimicking the on-off cycle of a tumble-drier, all because Mac—the man she'd given her heart to all those years ago—was sitting opposite her as if he'd never been away. But there was no warmth in his expression as their gazes locked. Instead, he was unsmiling and detached, like one of those beautiful marble statues that graced some of these very halls, as distant from her now as he'd been during the last painful six months they'd been together. They were some of the longest, loneliest, hardest months of her life, she recalled. Months when they were barely even speaking to each other, when they'd both sought relief and refuge elsewhere. Mac in his work—which was all-consuming at the best of times—and Tara in her dancing.

'Well, seeing as how you've gone to so much trouble to seek me out, you'd better tell me what you want.' He wasn't the only one who could project 'detached', she thought defiantly. The last thing she wanted him to conclude was that she was still missing him. But just seeing him again had brought so many long-buried emotions to the surface. Love, fear, bitterness and regret—feelings she'd tried so very hard to put behind her...and obviously failed miserably.

'What do I want?' A muscle ticked briefly in the

side of a lean, clean-shaven jaw that Tara remembered felt like rough velvet when she pressed her cheek to it. He also wore the same aftershave, she noted. A timeless, classic, sexy male fragrance that she always associated with Mac. 'I want a divorce, Tara. That's what I want.'

Her musings were roughly halted.

'You mean you want to get married again?' She could think of no other reason he'd finally got round to asking for the one thing they'd both avoided for the past five years. She steeled herself. He didn't reply straight away and, feeling her heartbeat throb loudly in her ears, Tara glanced round at the trickle of people moving in and out of the cafeteria, just to gain some precious time. Time when she could pretend he hadn't made the demand she'd never wanted to hear.

'I've met someone.'

Of course he had. Women were always drawn to Mac—like the proverbial bees to a honeypot. But he had always taken great pains to reassure Tara he only had eyes for her.

'I'm just surprised you haven't asked before now.' Pushing away her plate with the barely touched sandwich on it, she bit her lip to stem the threatening onrush of tears. There was no way on God's green earth that she was going to break down in front of him. He'd seen her at her lowest ebb and he'd walked away. *Walked away...*

Mac saw the colour drain from her face and wondered why. Their marriage had been over a long time ago, so she could hardly be shocked that he was finally drawing a line under it after all these years. In fact, he'd been more surprised that she hadn't contacted him first. He was so sure that some nice young man would snap her up the moment she'd been free of him that almost every day for the first year after they'd parted he'd dreaded the phone ringing or picking up his mail. Just in case it was Tara asking him for a divorce.

'There didn't seem much point until now.' He drew his fingers through his hair and Tara stared in shock at the slim platinum band he was still wearing. *Why on earth hadn't he taken it off?* Then she glanced down at its twin glinting up at her from her own slender finger and quickly folded her hands in her lap.

'So what's she like?' *Don't do this, Tara…don't torture yourself.* 'Your intended? Some single-minded career woman, no doubt—equally addicted to work with a designer wardrobe?'

'You should finish your sandwich. You don't want to risk passing out again. I won't be around next time to help you up.'

'Wasn't that the whole problem, Mac? You never were around when I needed you. Work always came first. Well, I hope it's brought all the success you dreamed of. Clearly it has if that suit you're wearing is any indication.'

'I never denied I was ambitious. You knew that from the first. But I worked hard for both of us, Tara. I'm not the selfish bastard you seem so eager to tag me as.'

'No. You were always generous, Macsen. With your money and your expensive gifts but not your time, as I recall.'

Silently he acknowledged the truth of her statement. God knew he'd regretted it when time after time he'd had to let her down—whether it was cancelling a dinner date, missing a long-planned theatre trip or sending her off on holiday alone because something important had come up at the last minute. That was the way of it in the advertising world. Everybody wanting something yesterday and unwilling to wait, because there was always another agency who would do it quicker or cheaper. He had worked hard to make his agency one of the best and most successful in the business. But he'd paid a high price. Some might say *too* high.

'Why did you move out of London to live with your aunt?'

'That's none of your damn business!'

Mac's gaze was steady. 'She told me you'd given up teaching to help her in the shop. It's a shame; you were always so passionate about your dancing.'

'Aunt Beth told you too much. And it's typical that you instantly infer any decision I make about my life must naturally be a wrong one.'

'Do I do that?' Looking genuinely puzzled, Mac slowly shook his head. 'That's not what I meant to imply at all. I was just surprised you'd given up something you so clearly loved.'

'Yes, well, you'd know all about that, wouldn't you? So tell me, what made you decide to try again? At marriage, I mean? Last time we were together you yelled at me that it was the biggest mistake of your life.'

The pain in Tara's throat was making it difficult to speak. He'd wounded her deeply with his cruel, angry words then walked out without giving her a chance to make things right. The following day he'd rung to say he was leaving. He'd come home that night to pack, then left her in pieces while he walked calmly out the door. A few days later he'd sent her a cheque for some outrageously large amount in a card with a Monet painting on the front—the one with the waterlilies—

and she'd torn it up along with the cheque and thrown it in the bin.

'I lost my father last year to cancer.' Mac's words were hesitant, measured, and Tara's foolish heart turned over at the flash of pain in his deep blue eyes, but she'd never met his parents. Mac had always been too busy to arrange it. Another casualty of his drive to succeed. 'Something like that…the death of a parent…makes you think about your own mortality. I'm thirty-eight years old, Tara, and I want a child. I want the chance to be a father.'

'Is that right?' Her words were barely above a whisper and Mac could see that she was visibly shaken. He frowned. A memory returned that jolted him. Clearly he should have chosen his words more carefully.

'I've got to go.' Gathering up her jacket from the spare chair between them, Tara got hurriedly to her feet. 'I've just remembered I've got several things to do today. I can't stay here chatting. You can have your divorce, Mac. You know where I live, so send the papers there and I'll sign them. Good luck.'

'Tara!'

He pursued her from the cafeteria into a long, echoing corridor with marble busts of grave historical dignitaries looking on and a shiny parquet floor. When he caught up with her, urgently spinning her round to face him, it distressed him intensely that she was crying. Two slow wet tracks trickled down her face onto her chin. Impatiently she scrubbed them away. 'What is it? You've got what you wanted, haven't you? What more do you want?'

'I want to know why you're crying.' He held onto her arm when she would have tugged it free and felt it suddenly grow limp in his hand.

'You said you wanted a child, that you wanted to be a father?' Suddenly weary and angry and beyond caring that she was about to lay her soul bare for him to trample all over it, Tara lifted her head and looked him straight in the eye. 'I begged you to let me have a baby...do you remember that?'

Mac did. He remembered a night of the sweetest, most erotic lovemaking known to man—a night that had come about after another bitter argument, when their mutual desire and attraction was stronger than the anger that raged between them—and his beautiful green-eyed wife laying her head on his chest and asking him if he could guess what she wanted more than anything else in the world. Suddenly his chest was so tight he could hardly breathe.

'I remember.' Hot colour crept up his neck and he let go of her arm.

'When we broke up I was pregnant.'

Her words sliced through him, knocking his world off its axis.

'I didn't— Why didn't you tell me?'

'Why should I have? You left. Our marriage was over. You didn't want a baby anyway. You didn't know if you were cut out to be a father, wasn't that what you said at the time? Work was too demanding, you were busy building up the business... ''safeguarding'' our future, that's what you said. Didn't that just turn out to be the biggest joke of all?'

'Tara, I...' Loosening his tie, Mac dragged his fingers shakily through the blunt-cut ends of his thick blond hair. 'What happened?'

Fear clouded his impossibly blue eyes and just for a moment or two Tara considered softening the blow.

She didn't know how, but she would have done so if she could. Cruelty just wasn't in her nature.

'What happened?' Her even white teeth bit briefly into her quivering lower lip. 'The baby died in my womb at six months.'

'Dear God!' Mac's exclamation was like a hissed breath. He moved away, shaking his head, staring down at the floor as if he didn't want to hear any more. Couldn't handle hearing any more.

'The baby was a boy.' Tara's sorrowful green gaze sought him out, made him look at her. 'We had a son, Macsen. A little baby boy.' And with that, she ran down the shiny corridor, the heels of her sandals echoing like cannon fire in her ears as she frantically sought out the exit, her heart beating fit to burst.

'Where shall we eat tonight, darling?' Amelie Duvall finished putting the final careful touches to her make-up, took a brief inventory of her appearance in her classic 'little black dress' in one of the two mirrored wardrobes that banked the big scroll bed, then reached inside her black sequinned purse for some perfume. Spraying it liberally behind her ears, her knees, then behind her wrists, she returned the bottle to her purse then threw it onto the bed.

'Macsen? I asked you a question. Were you even listening?' Barefooted, the French girl padded out into the living room, coming to an abrupt halt when she saw Mac seated on the sofa, hunched over a glass of what she immediately guessed to be brandy. He'd removed his tie, his hair was dishevelled—as if he'd been ceaselessly running his fingers through it—and the expression on his stunningly handsome face was nothing short of grim.

'But you are not even ready to go out.' Amelie could not mask her disappointment. She loved the opportunity to dress up and go out to dinner with her handsome escort—knew without doubt that they made an eye-catching pair, her own dark beauty a perfect foil for his blond Viking good looks. Whatever had brought on this dark mood of his Amelie saw it as her mission to shake him out of it.

'I don't feel like going out to dinner tonight.' Mac finally looked up at her, his gaze cursory—without pleasure—as if all his senses were deadened to her svelte Gallic beauty, then, tipping back his glass, drank down the remaining contents in one deep draught.

'But you said on the phone—'

'Forget what I said!' Rising to his feet, he restlessly paced the room then went to stare out of the panoramic window at the lights of London winking all around him in the darkened sky.

'Darling, what is the matter? Did something bad happen at work? A deal fell through, perhaps? Please put it behind you, *chéri*, tomorrow is another day. You will do better then.'

Sensing her moving behind him, Mac was unaccountably enraged. All of a sudden her expensive French perfume was too cloying—oppressive almost—and he wanted to tell her to just leave him the hell alone. But he wouldn't do that. He wouldn't resort to anger when what he needed to do was just come clean. Be honest. Stop this charade now before another relationship went to hell in a handbasket. It was bad enough that he was going to call the whole thing off. Since the moment he'd seen Tara today—even before she'd told him about the baby, *his son*—he knew in his heart he didn't want to marry Amelie. *Couldn't* marry her.

'Look...I know we talked about the possibility of us getting married, but all things considered—I honestly don't think it would work.'

'You mean your wife would not agree to the divorce?'

It was typical of Amelie that she would immediately lay the blame for his decision on someone else.

Sighing, Mac continued to stare out of the window. He thought about the baby—the son he'd never known—about Tara willing to face a pregnancy she thought he wanted no part of, then losing the child in the most horrendous way... His stomach knotted painfully with sickness and regret. 'My decision has nothing to do with that. I'd do anything to prevent you feeling hurt and disappointed, Amelie, but it's better that we end things now than go through with a marriage that would be a complete fiction. I'm sure if you're absolutely honest with yourself you don't really want to marry me either.' Slowly he turned away from the window to face her.

Her pretty elfin face with her wide doe-like brown eyes stared back at him as if he'd suddenly been inflicted with some desperate malady. 'Of course I want to marry you. Are you crazy? I love you!'

'Do you?'

She had the grace to colour a little. Mac responded with a sardonic little smile.

'You love my money, *chérie*. You love what I can buy for you; clothes, jewellery, perfume...' His nostrils flared a little, a memory coming out of nowhere that almost floored him. Tara's scent—a subtle, flowery, honeysuckle and vanilla whisper that had driven him almost mindless with need. He had sensed it today, even as he told her he wanted a divorce, and hadn't been able to ignore it. His body had hardened almost instantly. 'This proposed marriage of ours wouldn't really suit either of us. You are too young and too pretty to tie yourself down to one man and I...well, up until now my work has been my life. I don't deny it's important but now I'm ready for a family. I want to have children. I'm not interested in dining out at the best restaurants every night or flying out to New York or Paris on a whim just so that my girlfriend can shop. I want a home life. A *proper* home life.'

The French girl sniffed, prettily, with elegance—the way she did everything else. 'You make me sound so shallow, Macsen. I am deeply hurt you do not want to marry me. I would give you babies—lots of them.' But even as she said the words there was a discernible stiffening of her slender, gamine frame that spoke volumes to Mac. She detested the idea. He hadn't brought up the subject before but now he knew without doubt he was doing the right thing by bringing the relationship to an end.

'I understand you better than you think I do.' He smiled again, pulling her into his arms, but the kiss he bestowed at the corner of her perfectly made-up mouth was nothing short of paternal. 'Don't worry, *chérie*. I won't let you leave empty-handed. I will give you more than enough to tide you over until your next wealthy suitor comes along...'

CHAPTER TWO

'TARA? What are you doing sitting here with all the lights out?'

Blinking at the sudden brightness that flooded the living room, Tara guiltily uncurled her legs from beneath her on the couch and pasted an automatic smile across her face. The slightest slip of the controlled mask she'd so carefully constructed to prevent Beth knowing how she really felt inside and her aunt would pounce on her weakness like a lion on a raw steak, demanding to know what she could do to put things right. Her help would be well-meaning, of course, but ultimately useless. This was one situation her ever-practical aunt definitely *wouldn't* be able to fix.

'I drifted off,' she lied in answer to the older woman's question. 'I locked up downstairs, fixed dinner, then came in here to relax.'

'Did you see Mac?' Her aunt threw her keys down on the little antique table just inside the door and stood, arms akimbo, in that brisk, no-nonsense, 'I'm in charge' way she had that reminded Tara of one of those TV cops about to conduct an interrogation.

'I saw him,' she replied carefully, tucking some stray blonde strands behind her ear. 'Why did you tell him where to find me?'

'Because he was charming and polite and concerned, and because in my opinion it's about time you two got some dialogue going—even if most of the blame lies squarely at his feet.' Beth Delaney, tall, slim, fifty-

21

something redhead with Irish temper to match, slipped off the tailored navy jacket of her suit and arranged it carefully on the back of a polished Edwardian chair.

'I haven't heard from him in five years, Beth, so I think you must have misinterpreted the ''concerned'' part. And as for dialogue, don't you think it's a little late for that?'

'It's *never* too late to talk, my darling. Your situation is just too ridiculous for words. Married but not married…in the usual cohabiting sense, of course. The pair of you need to sort it out.'

Tara took a deep breath and pushed herself to her feet. 'It's sorted. He's asked me for a divorce.'

'Oh.' For a moment or two Beth looked simply stunned. Which had to be a first as far as Tara was concerned. No one, but *no one* ever caught her aunt off-guard. Sharp as a tack from the age of two—so the family mythology went. 'And what did you say to that?' Back in charge, Beth absently fingered the single strand of exquisite pearls round her neck.

Emotion tightened Tara's throat. In her mind—the fevered jumble of thoughts that passed for logic—she told herself it was only natural Mac had found someone else. But a stubborn, hopeful, definitely *illogical* part of her had always clung to the tenuous belief that one day he might come back to her. As of today that belief had been cruelly swept away, like a lone leaf in the path of a cyclone.

'I agreed, of course. What more was there to say?'

'What more was there to…? I take it you told him about the baby?'

Dogged in the pursuit of truth, Beth didn't flinch from asking the tough questions.

'He's met someone. He wants to get married again

and start a family. In answer to your question, yes…I told him about the baby. In some respects I wish I hadn't.'

Tearing her anguished gaze away from her aunt, Tara swept past her to the door. Some might call her a coward but right now she couldn't take any more interrogation. All she wanted to do was unwind in a long, hot, scented bath and break her heart over Mac in private.

'Why not? He deserves to know the agony he put you through!'

'He was devastated, Beth. I saw it in his eyes. What's the point of us both being in agony?'

For once, Beth did not know how to answer her niece. Making a little 'tsking' noise with her tongue, she retrieved her jacket then reached out a hand to gently smooth Tara's fringe from her eyes.

'You're such a beautiful girl, my darling, you don't deserve to be so dreadfully unhappy. At your tender age you should be having the time of your life instead of being stuck working in a fusty old antique shop with an old bird like me!'

Tara smiled, her heart swelling with affection for the aunt who hadn't hesitated to offer her a place of refuge when Mac walked out on her. An aunt who'd given her not simply a home but a job too if she wanted it; who'd stood by her when times were at their toughest and held her hand all through that dreadful night in the hospital—weeping with her when Tara finally lost her precious babe.

'You're not old, Beth. Not in any way, shape or form. And as for having the time of my life, well…' Colouring helplessly, Tara momentarily forgot her deep sorrow at unhappy memories she'd rather not dwell on.

'I think I had that for the first two and a half years I was with Mac.'

'The man's a fool!' the older woman declared in disgust. 'I said it then and I'll say it again now. I wonder if he has even the slightest clue just what he walked away from?'

Mac pulled over into a lay-by to study the map once again. Satisfied he was on the right track, he wound down his window to breathe in some fresh country air. It was nearly autumn and the Indian summer that had lasted well into the first week of September was at last showing real signs of abating. Leaves were already scattered beneath the hedgerows and there was the scent of wood-smoke in the air. There was also a refreshing drop in the temperature that right now Mac found he welcomed. The cool air helped him think straight and God knew he'd done some thinking over the past three nights. He had the bags under his eyes to prove it. Flipping open the glove compartment, he delved inside for a photograph—a dog-eared colour print of Tara standing outside the Tower of London that he'd snapped years ago when they'd first met. Laughing back at him into his camera lens, she looked completely ravishing with her soft blonde hair, sparkling green eyes and pretty summer dress that moulded itself to her lithe, slim body. Mac had hardly been able to take his eyes off her and she'd been so sweet, insisting on paying for lunch and treating him when they both knew he was easily the more solvent of the two. But he had soon discovered Tara was like that: generous and loving to a fault. And Mac had lapped it up, the attention and the loving, like a man who'd been living underground all his days until he'd met her.

She'd brought light and joy and humour into his life, and the day he'd walked away from her had been the darkest of his life. Until she'd told him about the baby, that was...

The pain of that thought was like a knife ripping through his chest. Releasing a harsh, dizzying breath, Mac dropped the photograph onto the passenger seat beside him and started the ignition. There was a deep frown between his dark blond brows as he checked his mirror then navigated the silver Mercedes out onto the country road to continue his journey. If he'd calculated the distance just right, he should arrive in Tara's little market town round about lunch-time. He'd check into his hotel, get some directions from the desk clerk and go in search of Beth Delaney's antique shop, Memories are Made. Whether she liked it or not, Tara and he had some talking to do. He just hoped that she or her aunt wouldn't simply slam the door shut in his face and deny him the opportunity.

'You can badger me all you like, Mac Simmonsen, but I have absolutely no intention of telling you where Tara is. I made the mistake of doing that only a few days ago and she's been a different girl since you and she met up again. She took a long time to get over you...losing the baby—'

'God dammit, Beth! Why didn't someone tell me she was pregnant? As her husband, I had a right to know!' Glad that the little antique shop was helpfully empty of customers, Mac knew his temper was on a dangerously short rein. He could accept he'd been in the wrong. He wasn't so arrogant that he blamed Tara for keeping her pregnancy to herself—not when he'd walked out—not when he'd been the one who'd asserted he wasn't ready for fatherhood. But he did hold her family responsible for being so damned self-righteous that they couldn't even contact him on her behalf...especially in her hour of need.

Beth Delaney bristled. Her long topaz earrings shook alarmingly as she crossed her arms in front of her thin chest and squared up to the impressively built male in his perfect designer suit with blue eyes that would dazzle a less immune woman at twenty paces. But Beth prided herself on being stronger than that. Her beloved niece's well-being was her priority and no amount of hectoring or pleading would shake her conviction that right now Tara should keep well away from this man. Not that she could imagine the proud, self-contained, Mac Simmonsen pleading for anything.

'Let me remind you that you relinquished all your rights as a husband when you coldly and unfeelingly walked out on my niece as if she was less than nothing to you! You put your business and your ambition way above your relationship, and that's a fact. It's just a shame you deceived Tara by marrying her in the first place!'

'Deceived her?' His handsome brow furrowing, Mac's heart thudded heavily inside his chest.

'Yes, deceived her!' Beth reiterated angrily. 'You didn't want a wife! You must have known you weren't interested in a real marriage when your work so obviously came first. You deceived Tara by telling her you were doing it for her. She's a trusting soul, Mac. She believed every word you told her. No matter how many times you let her down—and believe me, I *know* there were many because she cried on the phone to me—she would still end up giving you the benefit of the doubt. "One day he won't have to work so hard," she'd tell me. ''One day Mac and I will be able to have a real holiday together somewhere wonderful.'' She worshipped the ground you walked on and what did you do to her?' Beth paused to inhale a deeply outraged breath. 'You walked away without so much as giving her a chance at a reconciliation. I'm not privy to all the details of what went wrong between you both, but the fact is you broke her heart. And when she lost that much loved, much longed-for baby of hers…you broke it all over again. I really think it's best for all concerned that you just turn around and leave. After all, it *is* what you do best, isn't it?'

He told himself he deserved the tongue-lashing Beth had given him but, even so, anger welled up inside his chest because she'd made his walking out on Tara seem so premeditated and cold when the truth was it was anything but. He'd anguished over his decision for days and days, unable to bear the sight of his lovely wife looking so desperately unhappy. At the time, Mac hadn't had a clue how to put things right between them—they had seemed to want different things and the gap between them had grown wider. The demands of his business had swallowed up most of his time—too much—a fact he now bitterly regretted. He should have paid more attention to his wife; shouldn't have left her alone for most of their married life. Somehow he'd fooled himself that she'd wait until he'd secured them the future he wanted for them; fooled himself that she'd understand why it wasn't practical for them to have children right then. One day he'd make it up to her, he'd promised himself. One day he'd give her everything she ever wanted… Well, he'd made his fortune but he'd lost the woman he'd loved—lost her long before he finally walked through the door and never looked back.

'Marriage doesn't come with an instruction manual, you know?' Sighing deeply, Mac glanced at Beth and speared his fingers frustratedly through his hair. 'I made a mess of things. I know that. Trouble is…we stopped communicating.' A self-deprecating little crease appeared between his brows. Something inside Beth melted a little.

'*I* stopped listening,' he continued. 'It's just a wonder that Tara stayed around as long as she did. As for the baby…' Those deep blue eyes of his that could be as icy as a Scandinavian winter shimmered with a vivid flash of pain. 'Did she think I'd abandon her when I found out she was pregnant?'

Beth examined the two gold rings on her fingers and shook her head. 'Perhaps she worried you might think she was trying to trap you into staying. I don't know, Mac, but, knowing Tara as I do, I'd say that had something to do with it. She tells me you want a divorce—that you're going to remarry?'

'No.' Mac stared past Beth at the row of grandfather clocks that were unanimously chiming the hour in a cacophony of bells and gongs. 'Amelie and I broke up.'

'I see.'

'She wasn't the right woman for me.'

'So what are you doing here, Mac? Why do you want to see Tara?'

'Is she seeing anyone right now?' He couldn't help himself. He just had to ask the one question that had been bothering him since he'd seen her at the museum. There was no way a beautiful girl like Tara would have spent the last five years alone—but it still made him feel sick with jealousy to think of her with some-one else.

'There's never been a shortage of interested young men lining up at the door to ask her out. What do *you* think, Mac?'

He was afraid to think, truth to tell. There was so much he didn't know about the girl he'd married. So much water under the bridge that stood between them. He could only guess at the kind of person she was now. All he had to go on was memory—and hope…there was always hope. A dimple appearing at the corner of his attractive mouth, he allowed himself a brief smile before replying. 'I think the male population of this town would have to be blind *not* to be interested in Tara. But you haven't answered my question, Beth. Is she in a serious relationship?'

'Is that why you're here, Mac? To try and win her back?' Cocking her head to one side, Beth considered the silent tussle going on behind those riveting blue eyes.

He laid his hand on the smooth, burnished surface of a ponderous Victorian dining table just to his left, in front of Beth's desk. 'You have some nice things here,' he commented, glancing around. It was amazing to him just how many antiques one could cram into such a relatively small space. Then he thought of Tara working here, in that same small space, day after day—when she should be dancing, maybe teaching in a school of her own. Once upon a time that had been her dream and Mac had vowed to himself he would help manifest it. He frowned as he remembered. 'We need to talk. That much I *do* know. What time will she be back?'

Beth flipped open the big red diary on her desk but

her gaze was deliberately vague. 'She won't be back until this evening. She's gone out for the day. Said she wasn't sure what time she'd be home. Perhaps you could come back another day?'

'No.' He was unequivocal about that. What he had to say to Tara couldn't wait. It was already five years overdue. 'Here's where I'm staying.' Retrieving a small business card from his jacket pocket, he laid it on top of the diary. 'I've taken a month's leave. I'm not in a hurry to go back to London if that's what you're wondering. Please tell Tara I called and I'd like to see her. Will you do that for me, Beth?'

He seemed so sincere, in earnest, that the older woman relented. She prayed she was doing the right thing.

'I'll tell her, Mac—but I can't promise she'll be in touch. You might just have to live with the fact that she might not ever want to speak to you again.'

'Just give her the message—that's all I ask. I'll be seeing you Beth...and thanks.'

With a little jangle of the doorbell, he closed the door behind him and strode away down the street. Beth picked up the gold-embossed business card he'd left on the desk with the name of the best hotel in town on it and for a moment or two clutched it speculatively to her chest. 'Oh, Tara,' she sighed.

'It was a great movie, wasn't it?'

Hating to burst his bubble, though action movies with buildings and people being blown up at every turn really *weren't* her thing, Tara grinned ruefully at the handsome young man who'd taken her to the cinema. Raj Singh was the adored son of Sanjay and Binnie—proprietors of her local newsagents—and from time to time Tara and he would date, although their association was on a unanimous friendship-only footing—which suited them both. After Mac, Tara just didn't do deep, meaningful relationships any more, and Raj was promised to a girl of his parents' choosing in an arranged marriage. The wedding would take place in three months' time at Christmas, when the whole family would decamp to Kerala on the Indian subcontinent for a traditional Indian ceremony. For a young man as westernised as Raj, Tara was enormously impressed that when it came to the question of marriage, he was willing to bow to the more traditional wishes of his family.

'It wasn't in the same league as Gone with the Wind,' she teased, 'but it was OK.'

'Gone with the wind?' Completely bewildered, Raj scratched his head.

'"Frankly, my dear—I don't give a damn."' Ring any bells?' Tara's mouth quirked in a smile. 'Obviously not. It was my mother's favourite film. I was named after the house that featured in the story.'

'Tara was the name of a house?'

'Forget it. Let's go and get a pizza, shall we?'

'Why do you get to choose what we eat? You know I'd prefer a burger!'

'I let you choose the film, didn't I?' she shouted at him over her shoulder.

'You are one bossy woman, you know that?' Raj hurried to keep up with the slender blonde spitfire as she pushed her way through the busy throng of humanity spilling into Leicester Square and hoped to God that his promised new wife would have just half as much spark. The last thing he wanted was some submissive little wallflower with no opinions other than her husband's.

'Pizza, then home,' he said firmly, knowing Tara would completely ignore the assumed authority in his voice. 'I promised your aunt I wouldn't get you back too late.'

Tara stopped dead in her tracks and swung round to face him, hands on hips. 'Well, more fool you, Raj Singh, because I want to go dancing!'

'You do?'

'I do.' And, although she was smiling and determined to have a good time, inside Tara's heart was aching because Mac had never—not even once—taken her to a nightclub to dance.

'I think that just about covers everything. If you can think of anything else, call me. You've got my number.' His business concluded, Mac replaced the receiver on its rest and swung his long legs onto the bed. Picking up the hardbacked book beside him on the nightstand, he flicked to the page he'd turned down at the corner then, adjusting the stack of pillows behind his head, proceeded to read where he'd left off earlier.

Five minutes later, having read the same two sentences at least ten times, Mac dropped the book beside him on the counterpane and with a harsh sound of exasperation dragged both hands back and forth through his thick blond hair. Unused to having time on his hands, time when he should be relaxing and enjoying himself, he concluded it was a sad state of affairs when a man didn't even remember how to participate in either of those two very necessary states. He was so used to working twelve- to fourteen-hour days, his body seemed to have lost the ability to relax when he wanted it to. Getting up, he strode over to the old-fashioned sash window, lifted the forest-green drape and glanced out at the deserted street below. The row of Tudor-fronted shops reminded him how historical this little town was. How appealing to the out-of-town visitor or tourist from abroad. But it was mid-afternoon and as quiet as the grave...too quiet. How did Tara stand it? Wasn't there anything about London she missed? Apart from the Victoria and Albert Museum and Sadler's Wells, that was? The capital city could be an unforgiving mistress with its noise, traffic jams and pollution, but Mac had to admit he loved it—missed it when he wasn't there. In the early days of their marriage, Tara had often talked about wanting to move to the country and Mac had put her off, promising to discuss it 'some time in the future' when he wasn't so busy—when the demands of his steadily growing business were perhaps less. He'd get someone in to run the agency for him, he'd told her—then it wouldn't matter that he didn't live close by; he could keep in touch by phone or fax, just show up for the important stuff. His ambition had been like a drug, he acknowledged now, shame churning his insides. He'd let it blind him to the fact that his wife had needs too, and more often than not he wasn't meeting them. He shut his eyes at the memory. On the nightstand, the trill of the telephone mercifully jolted him.

'Yes?'

'Mr Simmonsen? I have a Mrs Simmonsen down here in the lobby to see you.'

A vein throbbed in his temple. For a moment he didn't know what to say. He'd begun to think she wasn't going to get in touch after all, as Beth had speculated she might not. All day he'd resisted the impulse to make his way back to the shop and see if she was there—find out if she was deliberately avoiding contact. Not that he'd let a little obstacle like that get in his way—there was far too much at stake for that...

'Tell her I'll be right down.'

As he descended the thickly carpeted staircase to the floor below, Mac straightened his tie, rubbed a hand round his recently shaven jaw, and mused that it was surely a good sign that Tara was still using his name when she could have so easily reverted to her maiden name. Even though they weren't actually divorced, who could have blamed her under the circumstances? But, that aside, he couldn't deny the throb of pleasure that pulsed through him at the sight of her sitting on the big cream sofa in the lobby. She was wearing light blue jeans with a crisp white blouse and she'd folded her tan-coloured jacket across her lap. She looked fresh-faced and pretty and when she trained her wary green gaze his way Mac knew an almost irresistible desire to get her alone, in the most intimate situation he could think of.

She got to her feet as he drew level, and her scent drifted round him, stirring memories strictly of the bedroom variety.

'I got your message. I can't stay long—I'm helping Beth with a stock inventory. What is it, Mac? What was so urgent that you couldn't just tell me on the phone?'

Going for broke, he squared his shoulders. 'I've decided I don't want a divorce after all,' he replied evenly.

'You don't?' Big as saucers, Tara's green eyes were visibly apprehensive. 'Then...then what *do* you want?'

'I want *you*, Tara...back in my life. I want us to have a proper marriage.'

CHAPTER THREE

TARA heard what Mac said but wondered crazily if she'd imagined it. All the way to his hotel she'd been frantic with nerves; terrified but excited at the thought of seeing him again—acknowledging that their unexpected encounter in the museum had stirred up so many hopes and dreams that she really should have let go of long ago. Especially after what had happened... But now, staring up into a fathomless blue gaze that clearly had no intention of letting her off the hook—not even for a second—she clutched her jacket to her chest and remembered that the only feelings she should have towards him were ambivalent at best—hostile at worst.

'Is this some kind of bad joke? Because if it is, I really don't appreciate it. One minute you're telling me you've met someone and you want a divorce, the next... What's going on, Mac?'

He told himself to take it easy, not to push so hard or he'd more than likely frighten her away for good. His insides clenched at the thought. Now that he'd seen her again he knew what he was doing was right. It was actually a shock to him that he'd survived so long without her. Maybe not so much survived as *existed*. How could he have contemplated for even a second marrying someone like Amelie? The French girl didn't even let her guard down in bed; she was far too obsessed with her appearance, too controlled to get low down and dirty, too...too cold. Mac only had to glance at the hectic colour seeping into Tara's cheeks to remember how warm his wife had been in that department—an erotic revelation of passion and fire.

'It's not a joke, Tara. Amelie and I broke up.'

A sharp spasm of jealousy coiled through her at the mention of his girlfriend's name. Before she had a name the woman had been a hazy nothing in her mind. 'Amelie' made her flesh and blood, real, and that hurt.

'So what am I? Any port in a storm?'

'Of course not.' He looked offended. Too bad, Tara thought wildly, when he didn't seem to care what he did to hurt her.

'We got along once upon a time,' Mac continued, sliding a hand into a pocket of his dark blue suit. 'Is it so crazy to imagine we might get along again?'

'You're serious about this, aren't you?' Inside her chest, Tara's heart was beating double time. Of all the reasons Mac could have given for why he wanted to meet up with her, a reconciliation was the furthest— the *last* thing in the whole wide world she could have imagined. What was behind it, she wondered, and why was he torturing her like this when the mere sight of him was tying her insides into some kind of intricate macramé?

'So serious I've taken a month's leave of absence.'

'Well, that must be a first! Are you sure they can spare you, Mac? I always thought you were so indispensable.'

To her surprise, a self-deprecating little grin hijacked his perfect mouth. 'So did I. Obviously that's not the case. Fortunately I have some good people working for me—people I can trust to do a good job. I really have no worries about being absent for a month.'

'And what will you do with all that free time, Mac?'

Tara asked, tucking a stray blonde strand behind her ear. 'Maybe some therapy might be a good idea?'

'Therapy?'

'For your workaholism...or are you still in denial?'

He could hear the hurt in her voice, the anger behind the bitter accusation, and regret twisted through Mac at the pain he must have caused her when time after time he'd put his working commitments before his relationship. Sighing heavily, he glanced round at the reception desk, at the interested glances they were getting from the smartly dressed brunette who sat behind it, who suddenly pretended to be looking at some paperwork.

'We can't talk here. Can we go somewhere?'

'Where do you suggest? Aunt Beth's shop? Your hotel room perhaps?' Her green-eyed gaze disdainful, Tara unfolded her tan jacket and slipped it on. Flipping her hair out from behind the collar, she bit down on her lip to stop it from quivering. 'You'll get over your break-up with your girlfriend. I'm sure you could charm her into patching things up—you always did have a way with women, didn't you, Mac?'

'What the hell is that supposed to mean?'

'Perhaps you weren't always working when you said you were. Perhaps you were seeing someone else when you walked out on me that night...'

Mac saw red. He had never cheated on Tara, nor felt any desire to. Sure, women came on to him, he wasn't blind—but neither was he promiscuous, and when he'd told Tara he had to work late at the office, well, that was exactly what he was doing.

'First you accuse me of workaholism—a label I'm quite willing to entertain, by the way, because it's probably true—but you go too far accusing me of having affairs with other women. What would have been my motive? You were always more than enough woman for me, Tara—don't pretend you can't remember...'

Coupled with his words, one glance from that suddenly heated blue gaze made Tara feel a surge of desire so strong that her knees nearly buckled beneath her. 'Well, I've changed! I'm not—I'm not interested in that side of things any more.' She blushed furiously, wanting the floor to open up and swallow her when Mac grinned knowingly and nodded. 'I have other more important things to think about,' she blustered on, 'I have a fulfilling job working for Aunt Beth, I have—'

'Why did you give up your dancing, by the way?'

Because right then the answer seemed to mysteriously evade her, Tara folded her arms across her chest and fixed Mac with an angry glare.

'That's none of your damn business! I'm a free agent now, remember? I don't have to explain anything to you. After five years I—'

'You're still my wife.' His voice was deadly serious—possessive, almost. Tara felt a little shiver dance down her spine.

'Well, we can soon remedy that. You've got some time off—why don't we find ourselves a solicitor and get some papers drawn up? Unless you've already done so, that is?'

'I told you before, Tara, and my assertion still stands. I don't want a divorce. I want a reconciliation. Understandably, you'll want some time to consider my wishes, but, as you rightly say, I've got plenty of time on my hands at the moment so I can give you my full, undivided attention. Why don't we start by having dinner together tonight?'

'I can't. I've got a date.' As she tossed her head, Tara's green eyes sparkled with triumph.

'A date?'

'With a man.'

'You're seeing someone?' The muscle in the side of Mac's impossibly beautiful cheekbone twitched tellingly.

'Is that so hard to believe?'

Mac glanced down at his watch, straightened his cuff then smiled beguilingly. Tara held her breath as every cell in her body seemed to throb and tingle.

'I'm not even going to dignify that with an answer. Cancel your date. Tell your ''friend'' that you're having dinner with your husband.'

'I will not!'

'Then give me his telephone number—I'll do it for you.'

'Don't be ridiculous!'

'Then I'll talk to Beth—perhaps she'll supply it for me?'

'Beth wouldn't do that. Look, Mac, this whole thing is completely crazy! We've been apart for too long. We're not the same people we were when we broke up—' Anguished, Tara breathed deeply, staring desperately down at the soft green carpet beneath their feet. When she was more composed, she lifted her head to look at him pleadingly. 'Go back to London. Ring Amelie. Believe me, Mac, a reconciliation between us just wouldn't work.'

'What if I said I wanted us to try for another baby?'

With a gasp of disbelief, Tara turned and stumbled out of the hotel.

Mac got into his Mercedes and drove. He didn't know where he was going, nor did he particularly care. All he knew was that he needed to breathe, needed to think, needed to get his head straight about Tara. He should never have said what he had about the baby—that much was clear. Besides, he'd gone at it like a bull at a gate and, unprepared, Tara had turned tail and run. Blaming her wasn't even an option, Mac thought as he negotiated a suddenly sharp curve in the road—he was the one who had acted like a selfish idiot. Right now she was probably wondering what the hell he was playing at. 'All right,' he said out loud, pressing a button on the dash for some music. 'I want her back. I don't care what I have to do to get her back. I want to make babies—lots of them. I want us to live happily ever after in a place of her choice... I want—' The words of the song that was playing on the radio suddenly penetrated his brain and halted the eager flow of words with bittersweet irony. 'It's too late, baby,' crooned the singer. Mac eased his foot off the accelerator and cursed harshly beneath his breath.

Switching off the offending record, he stared through the windscreen at the surrounding countryside with little pleasure. Give him the city any day, he thought irritably. At least he knew how to operate in the city. The countryside was too quiet, too...green, too—well, it made him introspective and right now Mac didn't know if that was a particularly good thing. He couldn't honestly say he liked what he was finding out about himself. Thirty-eight years old, owner and director of one of London's most successful advertising agencies, it was true—but that was where the success story ended. In every other respect he felt like a failure. He was a self-confessed workaholic who up until now lived to work. He'd walked out on his wife of three years because he'd put ambition before love and in five years had made no contact with her because he knew that walking out on her when she had desperately wanted to make a go of things—when she had *needed* him most—was pretty damn unforgivable. Even more so since he'd found out about the baby...

Half an hour later, emotionally drained and weary of his own incessant thoughts, Mac pulled over into a place signposted as an area of outstanding natural beauty, got out of the car and walked. Around him there was an infinite sea of rolling green, to his left a densely wooded area that with the sun glinting off it looked like a sentinel in the distance, and above him the bluest sky known to man. As he walked, his expensive Italian-made shoes cutting a swathe through the grass, the sun on his back, Mac surprisingly sensed some kind of peace descending on him. Shucking off his jacket and pulling off his tie, he continued to walk without looking back. A reluctant country-lover at best, he had to admit a grudging pleasure at this impromptu little foray into unknown territory.

'Any messages?'

The dark-haired receptionist glanced up at the gorgeous blond Viking who'd strolled through the doors of the select little hotel and almost choked on her biscuit. Flushing scarlet with embarrassment, she blinked wide-eyed into Mac's amused blue gaze.

'I'm sorry, Mr Simmonsen, I was just having my tea. Been enjoying the fresh air, have you?'

His immaculate white shirt was undone casually at the collar, his suit jacket thrown loosely across his arm, and intriguingly there were a couple of blades of grass in his mussed hair. Eileen Dunne felt one of her tropical moments coming on. With the back of her hand she fanned herself.

'It really is beautiful around here,' Mac replied, smiling, the dimple in his chin devastatingly in evidence.

Slack-jawed, Eileen cleared her throat. 'We have a lot of visitors who just come for the peace and quiet,' she managed before blushing furiously again.

'I can see why. So…no messages, then?' Preparing to move towards the staircase, Mac doubted there were but thought there was no harm in checking.

'There is one.' Eileen turned round to the row of little boxes behind her on the wall to retrieve a folded piece of paper from one of them. 'It's from someone named Tara. I hope you can read my writing. If not, I can tell you what she said.'

Staring at the opened scrap of paper, Mac felt a crazy leap of hope in his chest at what he read.

Mac.
    If your offer of dinner still stands, I'll meet you at your hotel at eight.

Tara.

'Thanks.' Slipping the note into his back pocket, he treated the awestruck Eileen to another drop-dead gorgeous smile then took the staircase up to his room two steps at a time.

'Thank *you*…' Eileen grinned at his back before taking another ravenous bite of her biscuit.

'Hey! What's all this, then? Going somewhere special?' Popping her head round the door of her niece's bedroom at just after seven that evening, Beth Delaney smiled at the colourful heap of clothing on the bed.

Tara was standing in front of an open wardrobe, dressed in one of those floaty Indian cotton summer dresses that made her look as if she'd just stepped out of the pages of *A Midsummer Night's Dream*—especially as her feet were bare. Her soft blonde hair was newly washed and dried and her pretty face was flushed from the recent heat of the hair-dryer.

'I'm meeting Mac for dinner.' Thinking it was best not to turn around just then to gauge her aunt's expression, Tara gazed unseeingly at the contents of her wardrobe, not certain about the dress she had chosen.

'You are?'

'I am.'

'What's brought all this on? I thought you swore you were never going to see him again when you ran into the shop this afternoon? Did he or did he not make you cry?'

Tara turned slowly to face her aunt. The older woman's expression was bewildered and concerned. She sighed. Right now Tara was feeling more stunned than if a brick had been dropped on her head from a great height. 'I want us to try for another baby,' Mac had said, as cool as a cucumber—while in contrast she'd felt as if her heart would pound clear out of her chest.

'I'm feeling very emotional right now. I don't rightly know what's going on with me and Mac. If nothing else, we have some unfinished business to discuss. That's why we're having dinner together.'

'Does this ''unfinished business'' concern the pair of you getting a divorce?' Beth asked.

Turning back to her vague perusal of the contents of her wardrobe, Tara sighed again. 'Probably.'

'Probably?'

'You may as well say it, Beth. You think I'm a fool for agreeing to see him again. You think he's up to no good. You think he's going to break my heart. Well, I've got news for you—he can't do it again because it hasn't been mended in the interim, so I'm perfectly safe from that particular affliction!' Her eyes filling with tears, Tara dashed them impatiently away with the heel of her hand. It was probably a huge mistake to see Mac again but she had to know what was going on with him—why he was professing to want to take up where they'd left off; why he had said what he had about trying for another baby. Until she knew, the turmoil in her head would give her no peace.

'The man's already caused you more hurt than I can bear. You gave up everything when he walked out, your dancing, socialising, *living,* for God's sake! Everyday things that gave you pleasure. You gave it all up because of Mac—because you were in pain and hurting. I'm not saying he's a bad person, Tara. He clearly isn't. But he *is* a driven man. A man addicted to work. A man like Mac doesn't know how to make a relationship work—more to the point, he doesn't have the *time* to make it work. Go and have dinner with him. Tell him you want a divorce and you want it now, then let him go and get on with your life! And if that means leaving here and going somewhere you can teach dance—then so be it!'

Her normally pale cheeks flushed with the passion of her words, Beth abruptly turned and exited the room.

Heart pounding, Tara dropped down onto the bed, silently acknowledging the truth of what her aunt had said. When all was said and done, she trusted Beth. When her mother had died ten years ago and her father had remarried and moved away, Beth had willingly taken over the roles of mother, sister and friend. Clearly, Beth's affection for her ran deep. As far as Tara knew she couldn't make the same claim for Mac.

She hadn't eaten a thing. For several excruciating seconds more Mac watched her push her food round her plate, then, leaning forward, deliberately stilled the hand that held her fork with his own. 'I think you're meant to put the food onto the fork then put it into your mouth.'

Startled by his touch, by his bold blue eyes burning into hers, Tara felt her mouth drop open. Needing no more reaction than that, Mac stabbed some mange-tout with her fork and lifted it to her lips.

'You've got it,' he said softly as she helplessly began to chew. 'Now, tell me why you're not eating. I hope you're not doing anything stupid like trying to lose weight.'

She flinched at his censure and the ache in her throat made it almost impossible to swallow the meagre mouthful Mac had dropped into her mouth. Glancing round at the other diners in the intimately lit French restaurant, Tara wished she could feel as carefree and happy as most of them appeared to be. Laughing and talking with their companions, clearly out to enjoy themselves, they were all a million miles away from the tense, apprehensive little picture she knew she must make sitting opposite Mac.

'Of course I'm not dieting. The meal is delicious, I'm just—'

'Just?' A golden eyebrow quirked up towards the silky lock of hair that flopped sexily onto his forehead.

'I find it difficult to eat when I'm not relaxed—when I'm worried or tense.'

'I remember.' He said it as though the memory caused him pain. Touching his pristine white napkin to his lips, Mac leant back in his seat to study her. 'I'm sorry I've contributed to you not being relaxed but I'm not playing games here, Tara. I want us to get back together again, and this time to make it work.'

'You make it sound like a project you've got in mind. Is that going to be your approach, Mac? Treat me as if I'm one of your accounts? What are you going to do—allot me a certain amount of time to achieve the goal that you want? I might have guessed work would come into the equation at some point.' Bitterly, she pushed her plate away, raised her glass of wine to her lips and drank deeply. As the alcohol shot to her brain, she felt vindicated in her anger. Why should he sit there looking so damned cool and arrogant while her emotions were swirling around inside her like some mini-cyclone? Did he really expect her to welcome him back with open arms after what he'd done?

Fiddling with the little pearl pendant around her neck, Tara narrowed her gaze. 'There's no question of us getting back together, Mac. You walked out on me, remember? Just a couple of days ago you came to find me to ask for a divorce. Now you tell me your relationship with this Emily, or whatever her name is, is over and you've decided you want me after all. Next week you'll probably change your mind again. I haven't a clue what's going on inside your head and I don't much care because I'm not the simple little country bumpkin you seem to think I am! Leave me alone, Mac. Just leave me alone and go back to London, will you?'

His reactions like lightning when she would have

risen from the table, Mac leant forward and caught hold of her hand.

'Sit down, Tara. This isn't finished yet.'

'Yes, it is!' Uncaring how many heads turned to look, Tara wrenched her hand free and dropped back down into her seat. 'This is cruel,' she said quietly, green eyes huge and shimmering. 'We should have got a divorce when the marriage ended—made a clean break. We shouldn't have dragged it out for five years...what were we thinking of?'

Slowly resuming his own seat, Mac stared at her across the table. A soft-footed waiter stopped beside them to enquire if everything was all right. 'We're fine,' Mac responded tersely, not even momentarily pulling his gaze from Tara.

'Perhaps that's a question we both need to explore?' As he examined her lovely features one by one, drawn like a magnet to her softly parted mouth, those full, naturally pouting lips moist with wine, desire slid hot and heavy into his limbs. That was the thing about Tara. She never had to do or say anything special to turn him on. Everything about her was inexplicably erotic. From her slow, sweet smile to the way she moved her body with such effortless grace that heads turned to look, to the way she cried at a sad song or movie. Even when she was furious with him, her lip quivering and her gorgeous big eyes shooting little warning sparks of sizzling green fire—it all made Mac crazy with want.

'What are you saying?' Smoothing her hair back from her face—those impossibly soft blonde strands that he'd loved to run his fingers through—her voice turned unwittingly husky.

'I'm saying we probably have a lot more going for

us than you think. There was always one area of our marriage where we didn't seem to have any problems. Far from it, in fact.'

It was hard to believe he was smiling. Tara might be feeling weak-kneed and hot because looking at him made her ache for him in the most carnal way, but she still couldn't believe his arrogance. Just because he knew she was no more immune to the sexual chemistry between them than he was, he had no right to think he was playing some kind of trump card. Good God, she'd been celibate since he'd walked out the door—she'd remain celibate for another five years before she succumbed to that kind of temptation without a scruple.

'Sex isn't a particularly sound reason on which to base a marriage,' she said huffily, wishing she didn't sound like some priggish little virgin.

'I agree.' He flashed a deeply bone-melting smile, a weapon clearly designed to elicit the most devastating response, and Tara clenched her thighs tightly together beneath her dress to stop them from shaking.

'But great sex—mind-blowing, knee-trembling, all-night-long ''we don't need to sleep'' sex—now, that's another thing altogether. Wouldn't you agree?'

'If that's all you want from a marriage, you could pay a call-girl. I'm sure you could afford it. What could be better? No strings attached and no demands on your precious time—except when you wanted it.'

As soon as the words were out of her mouth, Tara immediately regretted them. She wasn't a bitch and had no aspirations to ever be one. But if she'd offended Mac, he gave her no indication; not so much as a twitch of an eyebrow.

'I told you what I want, Tara. I want a wife, children;

I want us to be a proper family. Don't you want that too? Once upon a time you did.'

'But you were the one who wasn't interested in having a family. You were the one who left when I was pregnant! Remember?'

'You should have told me.'

'Oh, and I suppose you would have stayed because of the baby? Even if I had to raise him more or less on my own, because when would you have played father? It was dark when you left the house in the morning and when you came home it was dark again—not to mention the fact you also worked most weekends. When would you have seen our child, Mac? When he was twenty-one?'

Twisting his hands together on the table-top, Mac raised his deep blue gaze to Tara's and she was shocked to see the sudden bleakness in his eyes. 'Tell me about him. About the baby.'

CHAPTER FOUR

'HE WAS beautiful…perfect…even though he was so tiny. They wrapped him in a blanket and let me hold him. He just looked as if—as if he was asleep.' Reaching for her wine glass, Tara took a deep gulp then wiped the back of her hand across her mouth. Mac saw her hands shake, her eyes swim with tears, and he wished they were alone so that he could take her in his arms and comfort her. Maybe she'd find it in her heart to comfort him as well, because he was hurting too. He'd honestly thought he was doing the best thing for them both when he left. All he'd been doing was making Tara more and more unhappy with each passing day. Understandably, she'd resented the huge amount of time he dedicated to his work and he was frustrated and angry that she would never see his point of view— no matter how many times he'd told her he was working hard for both of them. But it was strange how those very words now sounded so hollow.

'How long did they keep you in hospital?' God, it was hot in here. Hadn't they ever heard of air-conditioning? With a slightly unsteady hand he pulled the knot of his tie away from his collar and popped open the top button of his shirt.

'A night and a day. Look, Mac, I really don't want to talk about this right now.' Sniffing, Tara forked some more vegetable into her mouth and made herself eat it. So many times she'd imagined telling him about the baby—Gabriel, she'd named him, after the archangel who had a strong connection with pregnancy and childbirth, whose name meant 'God is my strength'. She'd needed plenty of that particular commodity after Mac left. Night after night she'd cried herself to sleep, wondering what he was doing, who he was with; whether he had found someone else, someone who wouldn't give him such a hard time about his work, someone who would appreciate him more. The only thing that had helped Tara keep it together was the fact she was carrying Mac's baby. When she'd lost that baby one terrible night nearly five years ago, she'd wondered how she was going to get through the rest of her life and stay sane. If it wasn't for the love and care she'd received in abundance from Beth, she really didn't know if she'd still be around today to talk about that dreadful time.

'I want to make it up to you, Tara. Will you let me try?'

'You can't bring our baby back.'

'No.' Not flinching from the stark accusation in her eyes, Mac stoically clenched his jaw and took his punishment. After all, didn't he deserve it? He'd read somewhere that for pregnant women and their babies to flourish it was best if they had a stable emotional environment. Tara had been distraught when he'd left—nowhere near stable emotionally. Was it his fault she'd miscarried their son?

'We should just let bygones be bygones. Put it all behind us. That's what I've been trying to do.' Feigning a brightness she plainly didn't feel, Tara somehow dredged up a smile then got to her feet. Playing the blame game wasn't a road she wanted to go down any more. It required too much energy and actually made her feel ill. Also, she wasn't blind to the fact that Mac appeared slightly under par himself. His looks were still to die for—no question—but he'd aged visibly since they'd parted. Tiny little grooves at the sides of those amazing blue eyes and faint signs of strain around his beautiful mouth attested to that.

'Where are you going?'

'I'm tired. I've been on my feet all day at work and I really need some rest. Do you mind?'

'You sure you're not rushing off to see someone else?' Mac hardly trusted himself to look at her he felt so angry.

'Someone else?' Her brows drew together in genuine puzzlement.

'You said earlier you had a date.'

'And I told you when we met up that he cancelled at the last minute.'

'I don't believe you.'

Tara sighed. He had every right not to, because she was lying. There'd been no other date and even contemplating using Raj as a handy excuse was unthinkable.

'I didn't really have a date at all, Mac. I was only trying to put off meeting with you. I'm sorry.'

'Let me pay the bill and I'll take you home.'

'That's not necessary, it's only just a little—'

'I said I'll take you home. Just wait a second, will you?' Reaching for his wallet, Mac signalled the waiter, his expression shuttered and cold. With a heavy heart, Tara collected her jacket and bag and went to the door of the restaurant to wait for him.

Was it possible for a day to be much greyer than this? Tara pondered glumly as she paused from polishing a grand old Victorian sideboard to stare forlornly out of the shop-front window. Rain was falling so heavily that it was thumping against the pavement like someone knocking seven bells out of a punch-bag. An intrepid shopper or two hurried by, umbrellas wavering, faces pinched as they scattered to get out of the rain, and Peter Trent—the serious-faced bookseller across the road—had just covered his outside book display with a tarpaulin. The poor man barely made enough to cover his costs as it was; it wasn't likely he'd get many customers today in this downpour. Especially not now the holiday season was over.

Rubbing her fingers against the side of her temple where the glimmerings of a headache was threatening, Tara ached to know what Mac was doing. It had been two days since they'd had dinner together and she'd had no contact from him since. 'I'll see you soon,' he'd said when he'd dropped her home that evening, but his distant expression hardly invited confidence and he'd stridden off into the night as though he had the worries of the world upon his powerful shoulders. Secretly, she would have given anything to help soothe those worries away, maybe massaging those very same powerful shoulders as she'd used to do for him when he was tired or stressed. He worked too hard and it was beginning to show. It was something when a man like Mac thought that relaxing meant going to the gym and pounding the treadmill or lifting weights. She'd tried to introduce him to the restorative powers of the countryside, but he had been moody and unresponsive on nearly every single attempt so in the end Tara used to wind up going on her own. Just as she'd done most things in their married life…alone.

Staring bleakly out at the teeming rain, Tara wondered if Mac had already gone back to London.

Perhaps trying for a reconciliation between them no longer held such appeal? Her heart turned over.

It would be for the best, she told herself sternly. They couldn't make things work the first time round—what made him think they'd be any better at it this time? And she certainly wasn't going back into a situation similar to what they'd had before, with Mac working all the hours God sent and herself at home alone and unhappy. Not that their rented state-of-the-art apartment in Docklands had ever felt like home. No. She was much better off here with Aunt Beth. Their little town might be a tad on the quiet side in comparison to what London had to offer but Mac could keep his teeming, polluted city where they'd never even got the chance to know their neighbours because they were working all the hours God sent too.

'What ghastly weather!' The heavy oak door at the end of the room creaked open and Beth appeared, carrying a small tray with two large purple mugs on it. Detecting the delicious aroma of French roast coffee, Tara left her duster on top of the sideboard she'd been halfheartedly polishing and went to retrieve one. 'Thanks for this. You must have read my mind.'

'It won't help your headache.'

'How did you know I've got a headache?'

Depositing the empty tray on a nearby chair, Beth pushed aside some papers on her desk then perched herself on the edge of it. Her long teardrop pearl earrings dangling against the burnished red curls of her hair, she took a sip of coffee then smiled knowingly at her niece.

'Because you've got that little frown between your brows that you always get when you're trying hard to focus. Why don't you pop into the kitchen and get some aspirin?'

Tara shrugged. 'I'll be fine. Don't you worry about me.'

'But I *do* worry about you, darling, and you know why. Have you heard from Mac?'

'No.' Nursing her mug of coffee in both hands, Tara strove to keep her expression as carefully bland as possible. 'For all I know, he's gone back to London.'

'That's hardly likely, sweetheart—not when I know how single-minded your husband can be when he wants something. Remember that big confectionery account that everyone was vying for about six years ago? Mac beat all the competition hands down to get it, and it wasn't just because of that handsome face of his either. He worked night and day to—'

'I know that, Beth. I was there, remember?' A little stab of hurt reverberated through Tara. There were nights when Mac hadn't come home at all during that particular campaign. He'd taken to sleeping on the couch in his office just so that he could be 'on hand' at the press of a telephone keypad, and if Tara had wanted to see him at all she'd had to practically make an appointment with his secretary—the ice-cool Amanda, who always managed to make her feel as if she was somehow bothering Mac or distracting him from something important.

Her memory of that particular time was an apt reminder of why her getting back together with Mac was a total impossibility. He might have professed to have taken a month's leave to pursue a reconciliation but as far as Tara could see there were no signs that work still wasn't a priority where he was concerned.

'And he's not my husband...at least not in the way

that matters.' Irked, Tara rubbed at her temple, her headache suddenly developing into something much more bothersome. 'I think I will go and get that aspirin after all.'

'I wouldn't rush off just yet if I were you,' Beth remarked, nodding towards the glass door that was the entrance to the shop. Crowding the narrow doorway, filling it with his broad shoulders and impressive height, was Mac. He was wearing a stylish grey mackintosh with a damp patch on the chest, and rain rolled off the big black umbrella he shook out then stood carefully against the outside wall. His light-coloured hair curled into the back of his collar, the rain glistening on his riveting, clean-cut features, making his blue eyes seem even bluer...*electric* blue. For Tara, time seemed to stand still. She barely even realised she was holding her breath until it expelled suddenly on a deeply heartfelt sigh. Clutching her coffee mug tightly as though it were some kind of life raft in a sea of great uncertainty, she wiped her free hand nervously down her jeans.

'Good morning,' Beth said cheerfully—*too* cheerfully for Tara's liking. 'You're just in time for some coffee. Black, no sugar, wasn't it?'

Negotiating his way past the ponderous Victorian sideboard, some chairs and a stately red and gold chaise longue that was definitely in the market for some loving restoration, Mac frowned in surprise. 'I'm flattered you remember.'

'I remember a lot of things about you, Mac Simmonsen. Some good...some not so good.' And with that Beth disappeared behind the creaking oak door, leaving Tara alone with Mac.

For several seconds neither of them spoke. For his

part, Mac just drank in the view. Dressed in light blue denim jeans and a mint-green cashmere sweater, a pair of small gold studs at her ears, Tara looked young and pretty—her appeal all the more potent on this rainy autumnal day when Mac had wondered gloomily if he was on a lost cause trying to win her back.

'So…how are you feeling today?' he asked.

'I'm fine,' she lied, wishing the incessant throbbing in her head would go away. 'I thought maybe you'd gone back to London.'

'Now, why would I do a thing like that?'

'Withdrawal symptoms from not being at work?' Lifting one eyebrow, Tara was disconcerted to see him smile. Mac not smiling was unsettling. Mac *smiling* was even more so.

'You wound me to the core.'

'I doubt it.' For some insane reason, she found herself smiling back at him. Blinking in disbelief, Mac felt as if he'd been winded. Seeing her smile was like a chink of ice breaking away from a frozen lake. Suddenly there was hope for better days to come. A flash of warmth coiled inside him like a wisp of smoke.

'I came in the hope of enticing you away for the afternoon.'

'Where to?' Tara's hand curled even more tightly round the bright purple mug. She should have just told him a straight 'no,' but the rain outside continued to fall like the onset of Noah's flood and something inside her ached for something good to happen. The fact that she was willing to associate Mac with something good didn't bear examination right then.

'Apparently there's a very good health club and spa not ten miles from here. I thought I might go use the gym and get a massage afterwards. You game?'

Oh, my... There was something highly erotic about the idea of Mac getting a massage. And what was it about the very word that made her tingle all over in sensual anticipation? 'You certainly do know how to tempt a girl,' she responded, trying hard to keep her tone light—not easy when Mac's heated examination of her face and figure was making her feel as if she could melt right into the floor.

'I *used* to,' he replied, his voice pitched huskily low, and Tara's mesmerised gaze locked hungrily with his, her hands itching to divest him of his expensive, stylish raincoat and whatever else he had on underneath it.

'So...are you going to join me?'

'I'll have to check with Beth first.'

'What's that, darling?' The lady in question suddenly appeared, another steaming mug of coffee transported carefully between her flawlessly manicured hands.

'Mac's invited me out for the afternoon...to a health spa. Can you spare me?'

Beth rolled her eyes. 'Does it look as if the customers are falling over each other to come in the door? Of course I can spare you. Go and enjoy yourself. A health spa, you say? You'd be stark, raving bonkers to pass up that kind of invitation!'

'Thanks, Beth.'

'It might help you get rid of that headache.'

'Headache?' Mac's interested gaze swung from Beth to Tara.

'It's practically gone,' she insisted, flushing guiltily.

His expression suddenly stern, Mac jerked his chin towards the door that Beth had just appeared from. 'Take some aspirin before we go. I take it you have eaten something this morning?'

'She said she wasn't hungry.' Beth frowned.

Mac's answering gaze was relentless. 'We're not going anywhere until you have a sandwich at least, and I'm going to sit there with you and make sure you eat it!'

For once, Beth could only agree with him. Her niece was looking a little thinner lately and she certainly didn't want her to lose any more weight. She herself was definitely not a supporter of the much purported adage 'thin is beautiful.' A woman with curves was much more attractive and, if Beth knew anything about men, the majority of them certainly went along with that.

'Let's go into the kitchen,' she suggested, smiling. 'Here, take your coffee, Mac, and I'll just lock up the shop for half an hour.'

A couple of hours later, wrapped in a soft white terrycloth robe after one of the most sumptuous, thorough and relaxing massages known to woman, Tara sat in the communal seating area for guests—'The Paradise Connection'—sipping an exotic organic cocktail of several different fruit juices and wondering what on earth she'd done lately to deserve such mind-blowing bliss. Mac still hadn't appeared from his own massage and so Tara could happily just let her mind wander, admire her heavenly surroundings with their sky-blue walls and various exotic shrubs and let the glorious mingled scents of essential oils wash over her like a balm.

Reaching over to a little rattan table, she carefully deposited her drink then scooped up a magazine and immersed herself in a diet of high fashion, mouth-watering food and glossy profiles of some leading

Hollywood actresses. 'Mind candy', but fun just the
same when Tara hardly ever spent time sitting down to
relax. She was nearly always on her feet. Her particular
favourite way of relaxing was tramping through the
countryside, rucksack on her back, a map and a com-
pass to guide her and the luxury of taking her own
sweet time to get to wherever she was headed—knowing only too well that it was the journey and not the
destination that was the important thing. If only she
had been able to persuade Mac of the pleasures that
could unfold on such a trip, but she'd never been able
to prise him away from work for long enough. All she
knew was that half an hour into her walk and all her
troubles blew away—even the worst ones. It was true
that nature was a wonderful healer and, living where
she did, just a few minutes away from the most breathtaking scenery and landscape, Tara knew she would
never again opt to live in a city.

'How's the headache?'

Green eyes widening in surprise, she glanced up to
find Mac grinning down at her. He too wore a white
terry robe and the places where his skin was inadvertently exposed glistened with traces of the sensual oils
that had been used in his massage. With his thick blond
hair slicked back from his face, and worry lines melted
away, he suddenly appeared years younger—boyish almost. Something tugged at Tara's heart and emotion
welled in her chest.

'What headache?' she breathed.

'So it was worth the trip out here?'

'Ten out of ten. It's got my vote.'

'Good.' Pulling a nearby rattan chair closer and
dropping down into it, he smiled deeply into her eyes.

'You clearly don't take enough time out to pamper yourself.'

'Look who's talking.'

Her suddenly shy green eyes were provoking all kinds of delicious responses in Mac's newly relaxed body. He wondered if she was naked beneath her robe and thought he would very much like to see his wife as nature intended once more. Well...not just once more. *For ever and ever till death us do part*—just as he had promised in their marriage vows. His chest tightened with sudden longing. No amount of success at work could compare with how he felt when he was with Tara. For a while there when they were first together, she'd made him feel like a better man. A *good* man. How had he so hopelessly lost sight of everything they'd had in preference for forging ahead in his career? In the advertising business they called him 'The Magician' because he had a reputation for making a success of even the most difficult accounts. The advertising campaigns he took charge of were innovative and thought-provoking as well as clever. 'Works of art,' one impressed business analyst in a national newspaper had commented. But as far as his marriage was concerned, Mac was nowhere near being a magician. More like the kiss of death, he thought, pained.

He'd gone very quiet and Tara was curious to know why. Yet again she thought she saw agitation in his eyes, and before she could consider the wisdom of such an action she put her hand on his knee and squeezed it a little. 'You're frowning,' she told him. 'What is it, Mac? What's on your mind?'

Glancing down at her pale, slender hand on his knee, Mac swallowed hard. She couldn't know that her touch was burning him, making him ache as though he would never stop—not until she touched him some more; not until they could be naked together in bed. Not until he'd assuaged himself of five years' worth of dreadful separation—then and only then would he feel whole again...*healed*.

'I've been thinking about going away for a while. Taking a holiday.'

'Oh.' Abruptly withdrawing her hand, Tara reacted as though she'd been scalded. Disappointment and hurt brought a lump to her throat. To cover her confusion, she flicked through the magazine on her lap, the colours melding and blurring in front of her eyes.

So much for getting back together...

'I'd like you to come with me.'

Her heart thudded as if she'd just missed a step. 'On holiday? Where?'

'Ireland. A friend of mine has a holiday home there. It's only a few yards from the sea. I can't guarantee warm weather or blue skies, but we'll have plenty of time to talk and stroll on the beach and get to know each other again.'

His intense blue eyes became the sole focus of Tara's surprised, hungry gaze. 'When were you thinking of going?'

Inwardly Mac breathed a sigh of relief. She hadn't said an out-and-out 'no' so there had to be hope.

'Tomorrow or the day after.' The sooner the better as far as he was concerned.

'And how long for?' Tara twisted a strand of silky blonde hair round her finger and let it go again.

'As long as we like. The house will be empty until Christmas.'

'Oh, Mac.' Suddenly agitated, Tara rose to her feet, walked across the room then turned to face him, her back to a bank of miniature palm trees in huge ceramic tubs, the smooth wooden floor blessedly cool beneath her tingling bare soles. 'Why don't we just put ourselves out of our misery and get a divorce? We're fooling ourselves if we think we can make it work between us again!'

Now it was Mac's turn to get to his feet. 'How do you know until we give it a proper chance? I still care for you, Tara. Why else would I want to try again?'

Crossing her arms in front of her chest, Tara was taken aback by the sincerity in his captivating voice.

'But you were going to marry someone else,' she reminded him softly, unable to keep the hurt from her voice.

His nostrils flared a little. 'No. I believe I would have come to my senses before I did anything as serious as that. Amelie really wasn't the marrying kind.'

'And you are?'

Her question hung suspended between them, like an axe poised to split a log in two. Briefly, Mac dipped his head. 'I screwed up, Tara. I made a mess of things. Aren't people allowed to make mistakes in that perfect little world you inhabit?'

Shamefaced, she nodded. Of course they were. God knew she'd made enough of them herself. She lifted her chin.

'All right. I'll come to Ireland. We'll talk, spend some time together...but I'm making no promises about anything and I'm going to have to insist on separate bedrooms.'

'That's your only stipulation?' Mac tried, but he couldn't in all honesty prevent the grin that started to hijack his mouth. He'd persuaded her to go to Ireland with him—would it really be so much of a stretch to believe that he could persuade her into his bed once they got there? She was fooling herself if she thought there was no chemistry between them any more. If the sexual sparks flying between them were visible, he knew they'd be glowing red-hot.

'I must need my head testing!' With a disparaging glance at Mac, she spun round on her heel and pushed through the double ranch-style doors that led back into the women's changing area.

CHAPTER FIVE

'TARA! You're going away...why didn't you tell me?'

Having sprinted the last hundred yards down the road when he'd spotted his friend outside her aunt's shop, Raj descended breathlessly on Tara as she heaved her suitcase into the back of Mac's silver Mercedes. Mac himself was checking out of his hotel and would be joining her any minute now with his own luggage.

Frowning, she pushed a drifting lock of blonde hair out of her face and regarded the tall, handsome Asian with concern. 'Why? Is anything the matter?'

'Nothing's the matter with me. I'm just upset you didn't tell me about your trip. I wouldn't have known about it at all if your aunt Beth hadn't mentioned it to my father. She said you are going to Ireland with a friend. Who is it? What "friend" are you going away with?'

It took a moment or two for his surprisingly possessive tone to sink in. When it did, Tara felt a distinct spurt of annoyance. It was taking all her courage as it was to risk two weeks in an isolated house with Mac on the Irish coast; the last thing she needed was for Raj to sound annoyed about it.

'As a matter of fact he was—*is* my husband. I'm sorry I didn't let you know before but I only found out about the trip myself two days ago. I was going to send you a postcard—a couple if you're good.'

For once, Raj didn't appreciate the pretty blonde's humour. He was feeling undeniably disgruntled that she was going away with another man. Of course he knew he was getting married himself soon, but he'd been hoping to enjoy at least another couple of months of Tara's company before he assumed the responsibilities of wedlock and all that entailed.

'Why are you going away with the man who deserted you so long ago? I didn't know you were seeing him again.'

Taking a moment to compose herself, Tara mentally counted to ten and slammed down the lid of the boot. The day promised to be unseasonably warm and she slipped the sunglasses on her head down over her eyes. 'My private business is just that, Raj, *private*. I don't feel the need to explain myself to anyone. Please respect that.'

'Now you've hurt my feelings.' He did a good impression of being mortally offended. 'I thought we were friends. Can't you understand that I care about you? And I don't trust this ''sometimes'' husband of yours—I don't trust him one little bit. If anything goes wrong while you're away he will have me to answer to when you get back!'

'Oh, Raj!' Laughing out loud at the unaccustomed macho stance he had unconsciously taken up, Tara threw her arms round her friend and hugged him tight. 'What would I do without you? You're so funny and sweet. You help keep me sane, you know.'

As Raj helplessly succumbed to her endearing manner, his own arms sweeping affectionately round her small, slender waist, neither of them noticed the tall, fair-haired man in the tailored black trousers and black polo-necked sweater who walked up beside the car, deposited his two smart suitcases on the pavement then regarded them both with suspicion in his icy blue eyes.

Raj saw him first and, sensing his withdrawal, Tara poked him playfully in the ribs. 'And let that be a lesson to you! You're not going to get rid of me so easily.'

'When you're quite finished, Tara, we have a plane to catch.'

At the sound of Mac's chilly tones, she let go of Raj and spun round, her normally pale cheeks bright with two hectic spots of colour.

'Mac! I didn't hear you come up.'

'Obviously.' A muscle jerked in the side of his jaw and Tara didn't need to be a fully paid-up member of Mensa to deduce that he was annoyed. Very annoyed.

'Let me introduce you,' she said quickly, wiping her hands nervously down her jeans. 'This is Raj—Raj Singh. He and I are—are friends.' Why did the plain, unadulterated truth suddenly sound so feeble? She didn't have a damn thing to feel guilty about where Raj was concerned but the way Mac was looking at her, he could have just walked in on them in bed together. Her stomach clenched angrily. He had no right—none whatsoever—to turn something that was perfectly innocent and good into something more questionable.

'How do you do?' Plain good manners overriding his sense of outrage, Mac extended his hand to the other man. Their hands clenched briefly then quickly dropped away—neither man exactly keen to prolong the tense exchange. 'I'm Macsen Simmonsen. Tara's husband.' He knew why he'd added that last and didn't much care that he was obviously staking his claim. His gut had felt sucker-punched when he'd crossed the road and seen Tara embracing the other man. Was he the date she'd supposedly not had the other night when they'd gone to dinner?

'You'd better take great care of her when you go away. She's very precious to me, you know,' Raj stated proudly, puffing out his chest a little. Tara would have laughed if the whole scenario weren't so intensely awkward but, with Mac's broad shoulders also visibly straightening beneath his black cashmere sweater and his eyes sufficiently wary for her to be on her guard, the less she said right now, the better.

'She's very precious to me too,' he said pointedly, breaking his gaze from the other man's to stare at Tara. She was grateful she had her sunglasses shielding her eyes because his words had electrified her with their sincerity. Surprised and elated all at the same time, she was suddenly excited at the previously anxious prospect of spending two weeks alone with him—'getting to know each other again.'

'Anyway, we'd better be on our way.' Glancing down at the gold watch encircling his wrist, Mac opened the boot to store his suitcases inside. 'We really do have a plane to catch. Ready, Tara?'

'I just need to say goodbye to Aunt Beth. Bye, Raj— I really will send you a postcard.'

'Hurry back,' he said meaningfully, uncaring that her husband was looking on.

'Take care of yourself too,' she murmured softly, before opening the door of Memories are Made and disappearing inside.

'So...is he the guy who cancelled your date the other night?' He'd waited until they'd boarded the plane and were seated before Mac returned to the subject that he'd been brooding on all through their drive to the airport. Head lowered, intent on fastening her seat belt, Tara glanced up at him in surprise. She'd guessed he'd been ruminating on something during their car journey but surely he didn't really think that she and Raj had some kind of romantic attachment? By the grave look in his electric blue eyes, Tara deduced that he did.

'I told you. I didn't really have a date at all. And for your information—' she yanked at the seat belt to loosen it a little before fastening it and blew out an irritated breath '—it's as I said—Raj and I are friends. Is that such a difficult concept for you to embrace, Mac?'

'The way he was looking at you was a little more than "friendly", Tara.' Mac tore his gaze away, his stomach muscles clenching at the very idea of another man desiring her. When they'd been apart it had been such an abstract idea that he was able to fool himself that it didn't matter if she was seeing somebody else because he'd had no contact with her. If he couldn't see her then it couldn't hurt. But now, having seen her—having inhaled her scent, her beguiling personal fragrance infused with the warmth of her body; having seen the myriad different greens that made up the colour of her beautiful eyes; having witnessed her smile, shy but unbelievably sexy—he just couldn't conceive of even allowing another man to come within six feet of her without his say-so. But he also knew she wouldn't welcome such unwarranted possessiveness when he'd been the one to walk out on their marriage in the first place.

'You're totally imagining things. In the first place, Raj isn't interested in me that way, and in the second...'

Mac met her mutinous green eyes and couldn't help smiling. Even if he was feeling jealous as hell.

'And in the second,' she reiterated, pausing to draw

breath, 'he's getting married at Christmas to a beautiful Indian girl in Kerala.'

'Then exactly what *is* your relationship with him? And don't tell me you're just ''friends'' again. You're a beautiful girl, why wouldn't he be interested in you? Even if he is engaged to someone else.'

'Don't you believe that men and women can be just friends?'

'In a word? No.' Shaking his head, Mac retrieved the glossy in-flight magazine from its designated pocket and began to flick through it. 'Sooner or later, sex always comes into it.'

A roar of blood thundered in Tara's ears. To prevent Mac witnessing the heat that suddenly flooded her cheeks at his reference to sex, she stared out of the small cabin window, thinking it wasn't only the fact that the plane was about to take flight that made her feel a long, long way from terra firma.

Mac woke up in a sweat, the last vestiges of a hear-trending dream tearing him apart—making his chest hurt, his heart pound. He'd heard a baby crying, a baby in distress. *Tara's baby? His son?* And he was inconsolable with grief because he was too late to save it...

Jackknifing up into a sitting position, he dragged his hands through his hair, faintly shocked at the sweat standing out on his forehead, the dryness of his mouth, the pain in his throat. He blinked hard, once, twice, then stared towards the window where the misty morning light was filtering in through the unshielded glass because he'd forgotten to draw the heavy velvet drapes closed last night. Slowly, he came to. When his heart had stopped pounding, he reached for the small bottle of mineral water on the nightstand and, opening it, drank thirstily. Glancing at the broad gold watch that still encircled his wrist, he registered that it was just past seven in the morning. He must have slept pretty deeply because he hadn't stirred all night since his head had touched the pillow around eleven. They'd got to the house quite late because they'd stopped in a nearby town for dinner and by the time they'd arrived—negotiating potentially treacherous winding roads in the dark to find the place—both he and Tara were too tired to do much else but find their respective rooms and go to bed.

Now, as he struggled to break the ties of sleep and wake properly, he inhaled a deep, steadying breath to ground himself. That dream had cut him to the quick and the feelings it had engendered still clung to him like the sticky gossamer of a spider's web. He just hoped it wouldn't return to haunt him later on in the day because he didn't think he could look Tara in the eye if it did.

Gazing round the room, he took stock of his new surroundings. Apart from his generously proportioned double bed with its quaintly old-fashioned patchwork quilt, there were two stately old wardrobes made of dark wood either side of the door, a matching dressing table and a rather appealing love seat upholstered with plush red velvet beneath the huge bare window.

Swinging his long, muscular legs onto the thickly carpeted floor, Mac got up, stretched and padded across to the window to inspect the view. His friend Mitch had promised that it was pretty spectacular and, as Mac's sleepy blue eyes focused on the ocean lapping gently onto a wide expanse of white sandy beach as far as the eye could see, he knew he hadn't lied. Sighing deeply, he folded his arms across his hard, muscled chest, silently acknowledging if he couldn't make his case to Tara for a reconciliation here, then surely he wouldn't be able to make it anywhere.

She felt like a child again, light and easy and free, unhindered by pain and regret and deep unhappiness. Kicking off her sandals and turning up the hems of her jeans, she ran barefoot into the white foaming surf, exclaiming out loud when the icy water washed over her feet and made her shudder. It was the most wonderful place she'd ever been to, she thought, glancing round herself in awe. There were green rolling hills to her back, with Mac's friend's lovely whitewashed house nestling amongst them, a cobalt-blue sky above and the vast Atlantic Ocean with its panoramic white sandy beach stretching for miles alongside it. Bliss. Briefly closing her eyes, Tara breathed deeply, inhaling the tangy salt sea air and the sound of seagulls squawking above, and knew she could never regret coming here—not even if there was no prospect of a happy ending for Mac and her in sight. Her eyes flew open at that. Mac. How were they going to cope with their sudden enforced 'togetherness' when they hadn't been able to cope all those years ago, when their feelings for each other still ran deep? Until Mac had abandoned her, of course... Had she been wrong not to tell him about the baby? Could things have been different between them if she had?

'Tara!'

She pivoted at the sound of her name, her heart bumping against her ribs at the sight of Mac, striding down the beach towards her, dressed casually in light blue jeans and a white T-shirt. The sun paid homage to his tall blond good looks, glinting off the rich gold strands of his hair and highlighting the firm set of his jaw and shoulders. Feeling suddenly self-conscious, Tara crossed her arms in front of her chest because she'd opted not to wear a bra under her faded denim shirt.

'Good morning. How did you sleep?'

Smiling at the surprising formality of her greeting, Mac stood back from the lapping surf, an odd little burst of pleasure in his chest at the sight of Tara barefooted in the water, her bright hair an eye-catching halo round her pretty face as she turned to face him.

'I slept well.' Apart from the dream… 'How about you?'

'After a fashion. Strange house and all—it takes a while to settle in. But this is fantastic, isn't it? It's so clear, like crystal!' She kicked at the water, laughing joyfully with childlike pleasure when it splashed up her legs, risking vulnerability because she momentarily forgot that Mac and she weren't close any more. Catching the sudden darkening of his deeply blue eyes, she stopped splashing, then turned back onto the sand to put some distance between them.

'What's the matter?' His voice rough with concern, Mac followed, digging his hands deep into his jean pockets.

'Nothing.'

'Tell me.'

'All right, then. I feel—I feel awkward with you.'

'Why? We were together for three years. We shared an apartment, a home…a *life* together. We did all the intimate everyday things that married people do.'

'And what about the five intervening years when we weren't together, Mac?' Impatiently shoving her hair back where the wind had whipped it into her eyes, Tara stared back at him, a small frown between her pale brows. 'Are we supposed to forget about that so easily?'

'No.' His expression was sombre. 'Isn't that why we're here now?'

'I don't know why I'm here. Put it down to a moment of madness. We've got nothing left to resolve, Mac. This is just a pretty distraction when what we really need to do is sign the divorce papers and get on with our respective lives.'

'No.' Something inside him baulked at her cynicism. He refused to countenance it and didn't like it one little bit. Especially not when he thought he might be responsible for its existence. Once upon a time she'd been the hopeful one. The one who'd always insisted the glass was half full and not half empty.

'No?' There was a little catch in her throat and Tara thought she might cry. Instead of giving vent to her resentment all she really wanted to do was beg him to hold her. To just once more give herself permission to experience the magic of being in his arms, to lay her head on his hard, warm chest and feel his heart beat. *Oh, Mac, how did things get so bad with us?*

'I've said it before and I'll say it again. I don't want a divorce. I want to show you that we can be good together again.'

'Of course. You have a reputation to keep, don't you? Mac Simmonsen, "the Magician". The man who can turn a lost cause into a going concern. Forgive me if I think you've got your work cut out on this particular "lost cause".' She jogged to where she'd left her sandals, slipped them on her feet, then started to jog away from him across the sand.

Mac swore softly beneath his breath. 'Where are you going?' he called after her.

'I'm starving!' she shouted back. 'I'm going back to the house to see if I can find some food.'

Tension easing out of his shoulders, Mac turned back to the ocean to stare broodingly out at the horizon. At least she hadn't said she was catching the next plane home…

'Hmm…generous friend.' Her green eyes wide at the stacked contents of the ample fridge, Tara withdrew a packet of bacon and a box of eggs. Rolling up her sleeves, she washed her hands beneath the hot tap, dried them on a handy tea towel, then dropped down onto her haunches to search the cupboards below for a frying pan.

Pausing in the doorway to the big family kitchen with its red checked curtains and gleaming stone-flagged floor, Mac stood and watched as she clattered about with pots and pans until she found what she was looking for. As she stood up—for the moment unaware of his gaze—Mac concluded it was certainly no hardship watching her slender yet shapely little body bustling round the cooker. And when she reached across to the window sill to grab a box of matches to light the stove, he saw the soft swell of her creamy breast press against the rough denim of her shirt and the heat in his body suddenly shifted urgently to his groin.

'Mitch said he'd have the fridge stocked for us. How about we cook breakfast together?'

Turning with the frying pan gripped firmly in her hand, Tara blinked at the arresting picture he made. Leaning against the door jamb, his tight jeans riding low on his masculine hips, the sleeves of his white

T-shirt hugging his lean, hard biceps, his blond hair in sexy disarray, he was a million miles away from the impeccably tailored, successful boss of a leading advertising agency, which was the picture he generally presented to the world. And with a little pang of regret, Tara wished she had seen him look so at ease and at home when they'd lived together.

'It's all right. I can do it myself. And we must pay your friend for the food. If you tell me how much, I'll make sure and give you my half.'

Mac checked his anger. She was so damn set on being so fiercely independent it was beginning to seriously bother him.

'It's all been taken care of. And you're not paying for a damn thing! I wanted you to come with me so don't even think about it. How do you like your eggs? Poached, fried or scrambled?' He came up beside her at the cooker, his blue eyes challenging her to come back at him with an argument.

Pathetically overwhelmed by his nearness, his sexy, musky cologne undoing her in every sense, Tara shoved the frying pan into his surprised hand and quickly moved away to the other side of the kitchen.

'You're the one with the incredible powers of deduction. Work it out, why don't you?'

They endured an uneasy truce as they ate breakfast together but at least Tara *ate*, and Mac felt as relieved about that as a mother fussing over a recalcitrant child who didn't eat properly. After they'd vacated the table and stacked the dishwasher together, Mac caught Tara's hand as she folded the tea towel over a wooden rail and turned to exit the kitchen.

'Why don't we go for a drive?'

Staring down at his big hand covering her small,

paler one, she felt as if a hundred volts of electricity had just shot up her arm.

'My preference is for a walk,' she replied croakily, disconcerted to see his lips form a smile. A very sexy 'I'm still hungry' kind of a smile, and she stared at the deep little groove in the centre of his chin and hoped she didn't look as terrified as she felt.

'Well…if that's your preference,' he drawled, evidently amused at something.

'But you hate walking!' she burst out, trembling when he didn't immediately let go of her hand. 'What's the point, you used to say—when you can take the car and get there so much quicker?'

'I said that?' Mac's brows drew together in mock horror. 'Clearly I wasn't in my right mind. I must have been in work mode. Hurrying to get somewhere.'

'A big meeting on the other side of town,' Tara recalled, blood roaring in her ears when Mac still didn't release her hand. 'You always had "big" meetings. Never little ones or medium-sized ones, and everything, but *everything* was "urgent". You led a crazy life, Mac.'

'I guess I can't deny it.' Scowling, he dropped her hand as if it were a hot potato.

Tara sighed. 'If you really want to go walking you'll need some proper footwear. Did you bring anything?'

'What? You think I'm incapable of organising the proper equipment for a stay in the country?'

'And I don't want to look at the time or have to hurry back. You haven't arranged to go anywhere else, have you? Or meet someone?' Flushed, because his smile hadn't yet returned, Tara had to force herself to stand her ground. Mac might not like what she was saying but, as far as she was concerned, he needed to hear it. She still wasn't convinced he wasn't the same work-obsessed man he'd been all those years ago, when he'd driven her to such despair.

'Look.' Without further preamble he removed his watch and set it on the table. 'I'll even leave this here. We'll walk all day if you want to and I won't complain. And in answer to your questions, no, I don't have to be anywhere else and neither have I arranged to meet anybody. No one else even knows I'm here, Tara. We can do what the hell we like, *when* we like.'

Wishing he could prove the validity of his statement and make mad, passionate love to her where she stood, Mac swept past her out of the room before sexual frustration drove him crazy.

'Mac?' Concerned that she might have offended him, Tara's heart thudded inside her chest.

'I'm going to get my walking boots!' he shouted back and she couldn't prevent the smile of joy that bubbled up inside her and made her bite her lip in secret delight.

CHAPTER SIX

'DON'T you just feel so much better being out in the open like this?' Pausing with one leg hoisted onto a stile, her cheeks glowing a healthy pink and her eyes as enthusiastic as a child's on a treasure hunt, Tara grinned happily at Mac, who'd been following her trail up hill and down dale—silently now for the past forty minutes at least.

Wiping away the thin sheen of sweat on his forehead with the back of his hand, he halted in the thick, tussocky grass with the sun warming his back and just looked at her. If there existed a sexier, sweeter, more desirable woman in all the land you wouldn't be able to prove it by him, he thought longingly. Talk about a honey trap. He'd been watching the swaying of her hips and that sexy rear end of hers encased in figure-hugging denim for miles now and he still wasn't tiring of the view. Even if his brand-new walking boots were giving him hell and he had a blister to end all blisters on the back of one heel.

'Give me a new pair of feet and I'd be on top of the world.'

'Is it your new boots?' Letting go of the stile, Tara tramped towards him, her expression concerned.

Things are looking up, Mac mused hopefully. This was the first time on the whole trip she was actually looking at him and not the scenery. He'd never had to compete with grass or trees before for a woman's attention and his male pride was taking just a little bit of a battering. 'Perhaps we could stop here and rest a while?'

'Don't you know better than to wear new boots on a long hike before breaking them in?'

'Hey,' he replied in protest, 'I'm a city guy. It's me who needs breaking in, not my boots.'

Trying not to display her frustration at having to stop when she was so enjoying herself, Tara considered Mac's plight and nodded slowly. This was a whole new experience for her, she realised—being the one in charge of a situation—and something in her heart twanged at the idea of a fit male specimen like Mac being in distress, even if it was only his feet!

'You'd better take them off and let me have a look how bad it is.'

Mac took a wary step away from her. 'No way! No way am I going to let you loose on my sore feet. I remember once when you tried to remove a splinter for me—you damn near killed me! As gentle as you might look, Tara—when it comes to tending to the sick and the wounded, you're more King Kong than Florence Nightingale!'

Mortified at first by his less than complimentary reference to a giant gorilla, Tara nevertheless suddenly saw the funny side of the situation. Mac looked genuinely horrified at the idea that she might tend to his wounds and, knowing that she did have a propensity for being a little heavy-handed at times, she clutched her stomach and let the laughter that was bubbling up inside her have free rein.

And suddenly Mac was joining in, their mingled hilarity piercing the haunting stillness of the beautiful autumn day. Then, as their laughter died, Tara was suddenly conscious of a new kind of stillness surrounding them; a stillness threaded with a more profound, elemental meaning. Endeavouring to keep her eyes on the khaki buttons of his flak jacket and failing almost immediately, she knew she ought to break the spell and move, put some distance between them before she did something she might regret. Something that could only bring her pain afterwards when she had time to consider such foolishness. But their shared laughter had made her drop her guard and now Mac was standing there looking like the answer to a needy woman's prayer with his gorgeous blond hair, stunning blue eyes and to-die-for physique. Not to mention a look on his face that was promising to give her anything she asked for...*anything*. Her gaze didn't stay on the buttons—it couldn't. When it drifted back up to his mouth then fell into that mesmerising sea of blue, her stomach felt as if it was tied in tight little intricate knots that she had no hope of unravelling any time soon and she ached in a way she hadn't ached since they'd last made love, all that long time ago.

'It's probably best not to take your boots off anyway.' Forcing herself to turn away, Tara tramped determinedly back to the stile, regret in every step and beset by a delicious kind of shivering she couldn't seem to still. 'It will be too hard to get them back on again. Best just make tracks.'

'Anyone ever suggest you join the SAS for commando training?' Mac quipped behind her.

'I really don't think the uniform would flatter me,' she bandied back then vaulted the stile into the field on the other side.

'It's such beautiful countryside...breathtaking.' Tara was musing out loud as she continued to walk at a fair pace across a bright meadow, Mac trailing after her, his handsome face intensely concentrated on the task in hand—getting back to Mitch's house with some skin left on his feet. 'No wonder it inspired so many writers and poets.'

'I'm glad you're enjoying it.' Stopping to draw breath, Mac watched Tara continue to walk and knew that he could summon up a sonnet or two after observing the graceful rhythm of her body for five or six miles. He was a fit man—regular use of the mini-gym he'd set up at home took care of that, plus a couple of long swims a week at his local health club when he could find the time—but Tara had stamina that had to be seen to be believed. Idly, he wondered if her ballet training had been responsible. He knew she used to do her exercises religiously before leaving for work each day. Her amazing suppleness had always turned him on—especially in bed... He uttered a quiet but passionate expletive and stared down at the tussocky grass, gathering his thoughts, trying to compose himself.

'Why have you stopped? Feet hurting?' she called across to him, absently lifting the weight of her soft blonde hair off the back of her neck.

'How much further is it?' he shouted back crossly.

'Time-wise I calculate about another twenty minutes.' Drawing the crumpled map of the area out of her jacket pocket, Tara peered at it, oblivious to the fact that Mac was having some considerable trouble in keeping his frustrations at bay. She appreciated that he was suffering some discomfort from his new walking boots, but other than that she was hoping he was getting some pleasure out of their long hike. At any rate, being outdoors certainly helped her cope with the astonishing reality of her being alone with Mac—on holiday together after such a long time apart—like a *real* husband and wife.

'Twenty minutes, hmm? Every one's going to feel more like ten.' Muttering irritably to himself, Mac rubbed his hand round a chiselled jaw he hadn't bothered to shave that morning, an occurrence that happened rarely, if ever, and flexed his toes inside the confining boots as if to test his agony.

'You can do it! Don't tell me a man who can quell a whole boardroom of advertising executives with just one withering glance from those icy blue eyes can't cope with a couple of little blisters?' Giggling out loud, Tara shoved the map back into her pocket and was just about to move off again when, ignoring the hot burst of pain from the back of his heel, Mac put on a sprint and headed right for her, like a runner springing from the starting block.

Too astounded to react swiftly enough, Tara just stared at him in disbelief, all the air punching from her lungs when Mac barrelled into her then, catching her firmly before she fell, urged her down carefully onto her back on the soft, sweet-smelling grass.

Straddling her with his long, muscular legs, his warm breath drifting across her face, he pinned her arms high above her head and smiled wickedly, the sort of smile that a pirate might deliver to his female captive...before ravishing her. Her face burning with a mixture of indignation and desire at such caveman antics, Tara lifted her knee and tried to retaliate in a most sensitive place, but Mac was too agile and too quick for her and merely tightened his grip with his own strong thighs.

'So...you take delight in torturing me, do you?'

'I did not torture anybody! Is it my fault that you

were stupid enough to wear brand-new walking boots?'
Green eyes shooting out little shards of emerald fury,
Tara tried to buck but her attempts to free herself were
ineffectual at best and, she quickly realised, futile. Mac
was wall-to-wall muscle and the sheer physical strength
of the man overwhelmed her. Overwhelmed her and
drew her, despite her vows never to let this man play
with her heart—or her body—again. 'All that desk
work must be making you soft, Mac,' she taunted and
wondered at her own surprising ability to be such a
masochist because suddenly the smile had gone from
Mac's compelling features and that tell-tale muscle in
the side of his shadowed cheek jerked warningly.

'No, baby,' he said quietly, so quietly she thought
she might have imagined the old endearment—an endearment he saved specifically for when they made
love. Goosebumps ran riot over her body. 'You're the
one who's soft. Soft like satin.' When he laid his hand
gently on her breast beneath her denim shirt, desire
jackknifed like a rope of fire from her breast to her
womb. The violence of it made her catch her breath.
He hadn't touched her in so long, *so long*…and now
she thought she might die if he stopped.

Easing out a button from its opening, he smoothed
the rough denim aside and slid his hand seductively
onto her perfect pale breast with its exact pink tip.

'Don't.'

The word came out when she didn't mean it but
something inside must have been trying to save her
from further heartache, to make her see sense. *Dammit*… Slowly Mac withdrew his hand, then his body,
and got carefully to his feet. Disappointment was like
a fever burning her up. For a few moments Tara just
lay there in the soft green grass, staring up at the per-

fectly blue sky, wanting to die. Then, as the slightly inclement breeze drifted across her exposed flesh, she pulled the seams of her shirt together, hastily did up the offending button and pushed herself to her feet.

Risking a quick glance at Mac, she shrugged and started to walk again. 'We'd better get back,' she threw over her shoulder. 'I think there's a good chance of rain.'

'So you're a meteorologist now as well?' he shot back from behind.

The corners of Tara's mouth eased up into a relieved smile. At least Mac hadn't lost his sense of humour. And, thinking of that potentially explosive little encounter just now in the grass—at least he didn't bear a grudge either.

Tara was in the shower. Knowing that fact and feeling unable to cope with just the thought of that curvy, slender body beneath the warm, reviving spray of which he'd so recently taken advantage himself, Mac made his way into the generous-sized living room to stare out at the awe-inspiring vista of sea, sand and sky. The view was truly something else. The sight of it seemed to reach right inside him to the place where not even he sometimes dared to dwell, swirling round emotional wounds and scars, hopes and dreams, like a cleansing wind challenging him to dream some more. Folding his arms across his black cashmere sweater, he couldn't help but sigh. Was he a fool to hope for more than this? This short time together trying to right past wrongs? To hope that Tara might find it in her heart to give him a second chance? They'd made a baby together—didn't that count for anything? Thinking about the baby—the son who had grown inside Tara's womb for six short months then died—Mac reluctantly remembered his dream. The sound of the infant crying so mournfully came back in an instant and the pain that swelled up inside him was unrelenting and totally unforgiving. Mac thumped his chest to release the breath that was suddenly trapped there, alarmed to find that his eyes were stinging with tears.

Angered by the emotion that washed over him, at his inability to control it—a skill he'd once prized so highly—he walked out the door onto the rectangular patio. Leaning against the waist-high stone wall that separated the house from the rolling panorama of green that dipped down to the sand then the sea, he took several deep breaths to calm himself, glancing up in surprise when he felt a few droplets of rain on his face. Just a few minutes ago there hadn't been a cloud in the sky. Now there were several little ones and one large grey mass moving ever so slowly but ever so purposefully overhead. She'd been right, the little minx. As he thought about Tara and their eventful morning's hike, Mac felt his skin growing warm. Throwing off the feeling of despair that had so suddenly sideswiped him, he turned and walked back into the house for shelter. Even as he moved the rain started to descend in big, fat drops. It splattered onto the patio and the potted plants that had a home there and he shivered as he stepped inside the living room, thankful that Mitch had also arranged for a basket of logs and some turf to be left in the utility room to light the fire. They'd certainly need it tonight.

'How are your feet?' Her blonde hair swathed turban-style in a big white towel, and dressed in white jeans and a light blue chambray shirt, Tara sauntered in, a becoming dimple at the side of her luscious pink mouth.

'Massacred, thanks to you.' Mac glanced down at his bare feet, at the matching set of blisters on his toes and heels, and promised himself that his boots would be well broken in before he ever even considered hiking a similar distance again.

Following his gaze, Tara strolled up beside him, leaning over a little to inspect the damage for herself.

'They don't look too bad. You'll live,' she announced brightly, then moved across the room to the big, inviting sofa with its myriad patterned and coloured cushions and its crocheted throw across the back. Making herself comfortable, she proceeded to unwrap the towel around her head and shake her damp hair loose.

'Is that all the sympathy I'm going to get?'

'Oh, for goodness' sake!' Exasperated, Tara speared her fingers through the heavy, damp strands of her hair and shook out the towel. 'Men are such little boys! If you had to endure half the things we women have to put up with you might have some grounds for receiving some sympathy!'

For some reason, her words didn't just glance off him in the way she'd obviously intended. She was right. Tara had endured the agonising loss of a baby—something that had been an integral part of her body, her psyche, for six whole months then was suddenly gone. On top of that she'd had to endure the physical agony of giving birth, knowing that at the end of it she wouldn't have a living child...

'Mac?' Dropping the towel onto the arm of the sofa, Tara frowned. 'What's the matter?'

He looked as if he'd seen a ghost, either that or

unexpectedly delved into a place in his mind where he didn't really want to go. Her heartbeat skittered a little.

'Did you have a funeral for the baby?' he asked, gravel-voiced.

Shock rolled over Tara. Her throat threatening to close, she stared down at her hands, focusing on her slim platinum wedding band as if compelled.

'I named him Gabriel,' she told him, glancing up. 'And yes, I did have a small ceremony, just me and Aunt Beth and a couple of friends. He has a headstone too...with all his details on.'

'That's good. Perhaps I can visit some time?' It was amazing he was able to get the words out without cracking, Mac thought desolately. Moving to the fireplace, he put out a hand to lean against the marble mantel. 'I'm sorry things couldn't have been different. I hadn't intended to walk out, you know...but things were a little crazy back then.'

Picking up the damp towel, Tara folded it across her arm and got to her feet. Her features appeared very pale.

'Crazy? It was hell! You know it and I know it. Something had to give. You probably did the right thing. I was the foolish one...the dreamer, holding on to nothing. We were both so unhappy and you took steps to put an end to our misery.'

'Only the misery didn't end there, did it, Tara? You were pregnant and alone. Then the baby died.' Moving away from the fireplace, Mac paced the room, feeling as if his legs were suddenly lead weights that didn't want to carry him. Stopping at the huge window, he stared out unseeingly at the view, taking no pleasure in it, his expression bleak.

'Things weren't easier for you when you left?'

Her question shocked him to his bones. Did she really believe that they were? He'd missed her with every cell in his body. Night-time was the worst. Used to having her beside him in bed, waking up and seeing her there, he felt as if he'd been bereaved when she wasn't. Once a good sleeper, he'd become a total insomniac, resorting to sleeping pills to try and get some rest at night to face the long, demanding days at work. He'd looked and felt like hell.

'No.' Gritting his teeth, he moved his head slowly from side to side. 'Things weren't easier.'

His expression said it all. Her chest feeling as if it was trapped in a vice, Tara clutched the damp towel to her shirt and wondered why people who once professed to love each other more than life itself could so easily let that love be destroyed. Mac's reply was a revelation to her. Somehow she'd convinced herself that he had got his life back on track pretty much straight away after leaving her. She'd died a hundred small deaths every day, imagining all the women that would now feel free to come on to him. Would he welcome them? Would he forget the long, passionate nights they'd spent in each other's arms so easily at the sight of another pretty face? Another warm body? Now he seemed to be telling her that he had suffered too. He hadn't left her for someone else—he'd simply been trying to find a way to end a situation that had become close to intolerable for both of them.

'I'm going to the bedroom to dry my hair. Perhaps we can think about doing something tonight? Maybe find a place where they have some music? What do you think?'

Mac turned round fully to face her. It was only because he knew her so well that he noticed the slight quiver of her lower lip that told him she was nervous. Was she afraid the olive branch she was tentatively holding out would be rejected? Didn't she know the fact that she was holding it out at all, and not catching the next flight home, gave him a tremendous surge of hope that he probably had no right to feel?

'I think that sounds good. The nearest village isn't far away. They're bound to have a pub or two…this is Ireland, right?'

'Good. That's settled, then.' Feeling a delicious warmth spreading right through her body because she had his smiling agreement, Tara tentatively smiled back then hurried from the room.

With a fine fire roaring in the grate and two glasses of creamy smooth Guinness placed squarely in front of them on the little wooden table, Tara and Mac made themselves at home in the unashamedly traditional Irish tavern and let the foot-tapping music of the flute and fiddle happily wash over them. When they'd entered the small, cosy interior of Paddy's Bar, the glances from the locals had been curious but not intrusive and the famous Irish reputation for warmth and friendliness hadn't disappointed either. The large, florid-faced barman—'call me Mike'—had bantered and joked with Mac and thrown several appreciative smiles Tara's way before leaving them to settle in by the fire and enjoy the night's entertainment. The two male musicians, one young, one old, the older one with a great bushy beard, played their respective instruments with a passion and a relish that made Tara think longingly of her dancing.

Hearing her sigh, Mac glanced across the table at her with concern. 'What's the matter?'

To Tara, observing him sitting there in his navy cable-knit sweater and snug black jeans, his newly washed hair gleaming in the firelight, Mac looked yummy enough to eat. In three years of marriage she'd hardly ever seen him so casually attired. Because he was nearly always at work, he mostly wore immaculately tailored suits, and with his pristine shirts, silk ties and expensive Italian shoes, Tara had often felt the clothes defined the man because somehow they seemed to put up a barrier between them that she often felt too unconfident to transgress. How often had she just longed to ruffle his feathers a little? To muss his hair before he left the flat in the morning, to loosen his tie and maybe leave a discreet little love-bite on his neck? To make him lose that rigid control he naturally assumed for himself. The only place she'd succeeded in doing that was bed, and when she had she'd been more than gratified by the result...

Colouring slightly at the direction of her thoughts, she took a brief sip of her drink before answering him.

'Nothing's the matter. This is great. The music just made me think about dancing, that's all.'

'Why did you give it up? Was it because you were pregnant? That wouldn't have stopped you teaching, would it? And please don't tell me to mind my own business because I want to know.'

'I lost my concentration.' As she tussled with a multitude of emotions, Tara's expression was torn. 'My nerve. You need joy inside you to dance, you know? And I felt empty, drained. Even more so after what happened to Gabriel... Working for Aunt Beth seemed a much safer option, plus I didn't want to stay in London.'

'And now?' Mac raised his glass, took a sip of his

drink and put it down again, his blue eyes watchful as a cat's.

'Now? I wouldn't go back to London if you gave me a million pounds.'

He'd expected as much. Now he knew for sure. 'And the teaching?'

'I've been thinking about looking for a post locally. There are a lot of private schools in the locality with lots of nicely brought-up young "gels" whose parents want them to learn ballet. It shouldn't be too much of a problem finding something.'

'What about the school you wanted? Your own school?'

'That takes time and money to organise. As you well know.' She rubbed her hands up and down her arms in the dusky pink sweater she wore as if she was uncomfortable with the subject, which she was.

'Why didn't you cash the cheques I sent you?' He'd sent two cheques because after six months had passed he'd realised to his bewilderment that she hadn't bothered to cash the first one. The same thing happened to the second.

'I didn't want your *conscience* money, that's why!' The heat of the fire making her scarlet cheeks even redder, Tara swallowed down her sudden spurt of anger and shook her head. 'I'm sorry. I shouldn't have said that. You were probably just trying to do the right thing.'

'Yeah,' Mac agreed soberly. 'Like I *always* know how to do the right thing. If I had done the right thing in the first place we wouldn't be in this God-awful mess!'

His pain and frustration tore at Tara's heartstrings. The man was clearly doing his best to make amends for what had happened in his own way and she wasn't even meeting him halfway. If she really was tired of playing the blame game then her words and her actions had to reflect that. The man deserved a break, if nothing else. Once upon a time he had been her whole world. She hadn't forgotten that, even if he had.

'Why don't we just sit back and enjoy the music? Better still, why don't we dance?' Her mouth trembled a little as she finished speaking but she stood up before he could register his surprise and Mac was still in shock when she slipped her hand into his and urged him to his feet.

'Don't look so worried,' she whispered next to his ear as she led him to the small area where one other couple had bravely taken to the floor. 'I'm not expecting you to be one of the cast members of Riverdance.'

Unable to hold back the grin that tugged at his lips, Mac pulled her gently and expertly into his arms as if he'd been doing it every day of his life. His heart was beating too hard, too fast, because he'd been longing to hold her like this ever since he'd seen her at the museum. Now that he had her, her blonde hair soft beneath his chin, her supple dancer's body pressed intimately next to his, Mac reflected that this must surely be one of those perfect moments that the universe conspired to bring humans every now and then...*if* they were lucky.

'Not bad,' Tara murmured softly as he led her round the room, to the slightly mournful tune 'The Maid of Culmore,' 'for a desk-bound city guy.'

The look he gave her in return was pure fire, pure need, and, tightening his arms possessively round her slender waist, he put his lips to her ear and whispered, 'There are other things this desk-bound city guy can do even better...if you'll just give him the chance.'

CHAPTER SEVEN

MAC stood in front of the fire, gazing deeply into the flickering, crackling flames. Outside the wind roared in gusts and the sea encroached onto the shore, waves licking greedily at the undisturbed white sand, although he'd drawn the curtains against the evidence, to shut out the night. From the kitchen he heard Tara humming as she went about making hot chocolate and for the first time since he couldn't remember when, Mac felt oddly at peace. Even though he knew the feeling wouldn't last—that the road to a possible reconciliation with his lovely wife was paved with rocks—he told himself to just enjoy the moment. Life, after all, was just a succession of moments when all was said and done and there were no guarantees—even though he might wish there were...

'You look very reflective standing there, like a blond, brooding Heathcliff—what's up?'

Her footfall was so soft Mac hadn't heard her come in. Gazing at her now as she carefully carried their drinks, he felt her pale, innocent beauty give him a little jolt inside. Their unexpected dance together in the tavern had only fuelled his desire for further contact and he was having trouble tempering the raw need inside him with the undoubtedly more sensible demand to proceed more cautiously.

But her comment made him smile. 'You always did have a wild imagination.'

Tara handed him his drink then turned away before

he saw the heat in her face. His words made her think of the hot nights, tangled sheets and sweet, erotic loving that they had once shared; loving that she still craved despite her vow not to cave in to the powerful attraction she harboured for her husband.

Beneath her sweater, her breasts ached at the memory. 'I had to have something to while away the long, lonely evenings when you weren't home,' she replied, then, placing her mug on the coffee-table, dropped down onto the sofa, drawing her jean-clad legs gracefully up beneath her.

'Do you really think I preferred being at work to being with you?' Leaving his drink on the mantelpiece, Mac dropped his hands to his hips and sighed deeply. 'There were a lot of major things going down. I needed to be there. My clients expected it...so did my staff. It's a myth that when you're the boss you don't have to work as hard—you have to work *harder* because people are relying on you. Anyway, things are a lot easier now. As I said, I have good people working for me. People I can rely on to take care of things. I don't have to show up every day if I don't want to.'

'Lucky you.' Reading between the lines, Tara thought she could still detect a heavy commitment to his job. There was no way she'd consider going back to him if that was still the case. Her heart grew heavy at the thought.

'Is this the line you're going to take the whole time? Antagonism?'

'Of course not.' Chided, she pushed her fingers agitatedly through her hair. 'But if you're serious about us getting back together, what compromises are you willing to make, Mac? The hours you put in at work were always the main bone of contention between us.

What's the point in being married if we hardly ever see each other?'

'I'd work a lot fewer hours.' His reply was immediate. 'And I'd be more flexible. We could take more holidays—'

'We only took one in three years of marriage,' Tara reminded him, 'and even then you flew back to London after only three days. I was in Bali, one of the most beautiful places in the world...on my *own*.'

'I wish you knew how much I regretted that.' Shaking his head, he stared back at the fire. He picked up the heavy poker and prodded the charred logs, watching the flames hiss and brighten in the grate. 'I can only promise you I wouldn't ever let that happen again.' Replacing the poker in its brass stand, he turned back to Tara. 'I want to be a good husband to you, Tara...and a good father to our children.'

Her throat tightened. 'It's too soon to talk about that.'

'Why?'

'Because it's hard enough coping with the idea of us getting back together again, never mind thinking about having children.'

'Are you scared?' he asked gently.

'Of what?' But Tara's heartbeat had accelerated wildly at the idea of being pregnant with Mac's child again. Sudden longing made her dizzy.

'Of being pregnant.'

What had happened to their first-born son remained unspoken between them, like an indelible hurt that would never go away but would always exist to haunt them with what could have been.

Restless and on edge, Tara got to her feet. 'What do you think?'

The Harlequin Reader Service® — Here's how it works:

Accepting your 2 free books and mystery gift places you under no obligation to buy anything. You may keep the books and gift and return the shipping statement marked "cancel." If you do not cancel, about a month later we'll send you 6 additional books and bill you just $3.80 each in the U.S., or $4.47 each in Canada, plus 25¢ shipping & handling per book and applicable taxes if any.* That's the complete price and — compared to cover prices of $4.50 each in the U.S. and $5.25 each in Canada — it's quite a bargain! You may cancel at any time, but if you choose to continue, every month we'll send you 6 more books, which you may either purchase at the discount price or return to us and cancel your subscription.

*Terms and prices subject to change without notice. Sales tax applicable in N.Y. Canadian residents will be charged applicable provincial taxes and GST. Credit or debit balances in a customer's account(s) may be offset by any other outstanding balance owed by or to the customer. Please allow 4 to 6 weeks for delivery.

If offer card is missing write to: Harlequin Reader Service, 3010 Walden Ave., P.O. Box 1867, Buffalo NY 14240-1867

NO POSTAGE
NECESSARY
IF MAILED
IN THE
UNITED STATES

BUSINESS REPLY MAIL
FIRST-CLASS MAIL   PERMIT NO. 717-003   BUFFALO, NY

POSTAGE WILL BE PAID BY ADDRESSEE

HARLEQUIN READER SERVICE
3010 WALDEN AVE
PO BOX 1867
BUFFALO NY 14240-9952

Get FREE BOOKS and a FREE GIFT when you play the...

LAS VEGAS GAME

Just scratch off the gold box with a coin. Then check below to see the gifts you get!

YES!
I have scratched off the gold box. Please send me my **2 FREE BOOKS** and **gift for which I qualify**. I understand that I am under no obligation to purchase any books as explained on the back of this card.

▼ DETACH AND MAIL CARD TODAY! ▼

306 HDL EFZZ　　　　　**106 HDL EFYQ**

FIRST NAME	LAST NAME

ADDRESS

APT.#	CITY

STATE/PROV.	ZIP/POSTAL CODE

(H-P-08/06)

7	7	7	**Worth TWO FREE BOOKS plus a BONUS Mystery Gift!**
🍒	🍒	🍒	**Worth TWO FREE BOOKS!**
🔔	🔔	♣	**TRY AGAIN!**

www.eHarlequin.com

Offer limited to one per household and not valid to current Harlequin Presents® subscribers. All orders subject to approval.

'This time I'd be there for you. All the way.' Slowly Mac approached her, a tender smile etched seductively on his beautiful face, his blue eyes dark. 'We'll get you the best doctors, the best care. You won't lack for anything.'

She was aching for him to hold her but she wouldn't make the first move. The fact that he'd left her once already loomed large in her mind and rejection was like a hundred tiny scores in her heart. Somehow, some way, Tara needed him to prove he meant what he said about wanting them to try again; that it wasn't just some whim of his fuelled by guilt about the baby they'd lost. And so far he hadn't mentioned anything about love.

'I couldn't move back to London. You know that?' Expelling a softly anxious breath, she gazed up at him with wide green eyes.

His smile remained. He reached out and fingered a strand of her hair. Heat swirled in her stomach.

'I'm not averse to moving to where you live now if that's what you want. When I do need to go into the office I can commute. We could look for a house, somewhere with a decent-sized garden so the children have space to run around.'

Oh, Mac… His words fell like soft rain on her dry soul. She swayed a little towards him, her lip quivering as she tried with all her might not to give way to tears.

'Will you let me hold you?' he asked, his voice low. 'Just hold you?'

Tara moved into his arms without a word. Urging her deep into his chest, Mac cupped the back of her head with one hand and circled her waist with the other. She smelled of flowers and sunshine and rain, all the things that nature manifested so freely and magically, and Mac remembered the slightly overpowering, heady scent that Amelie had favoured and knew in an instant the one that beguiled him more. Like the woman he held in his arms. Free of artifice, Tara had always had the power to beguile him from the very first moment he'd set eyes on her, sitting opposite him on a crowded London tube train, supposedly engrossed in a dance magazine. Only she wasn't. Not really—because she'd been stealing furtive little glances at him all the way from Oxford Circus to Victoria. When he'd followed her out onto the platform and waylaid her with 'What's your favourite food?' she'd automatically come back at him with 'Italian. Why?' and he'd proceeded to persuade her to have dinner with him that night at the best Italian restaurant he knew in London. When she'd accepted, he'd given her his business card just so she could check he was who he said he was, then walked back down the platform with such a feeling of elation in his heart because he knew without doubt that she'd be there at the restaurant at the allotted time. The electricity between them had been all but humming.

But right now Mac had no hope of proceeding cautiously as he'd so often admonished himself since seeing her again, not when his body had other more urgent ideas. Pressing his lips against her hair, he moved his hands up and down her back, loving the perfect fit she made in his arms, relishing the sexy, firm contours of her body, wishing he could just strip her of every stitch and take her here now on the Arran rug in front of the fire…

He heard her little heartfelt sigh then felt her tremble. Helpless to act in any other way, Mac tilted her chin up towards him to stare hungrily into her depthless green eyes with their pretty dark-blonde lashes.

'I never stopped wanting you,' he said huskily and Tara had the evidence to prove it pressing into her pelvis.

'Sex would only cloud the issue.' She shivered again but made no attempt to move out of his embrace. 'Nothing's been decided yet. I still—I still need time.'

'But I'm not suggesting we have sex,' Mac replied intriguingly and a spark of something like fire flashed in his eyes. 'I'm suggesting we make love. You'll agree there's a difference?' As he had done out in the meadow earlier on in the day, he slid his hand possessively onto her breast shielded by her soft wool sweater and cupped it. As he teased her nipple, she felt it bead beneath his touch into an exquisitely tight, aching nub. Tara's womb responded with a deep contraction. Hot little ripples of need pulsed through her body. The sensual pull of his fascinating mouth seemed to lure her lips closer. With a hungry little groan she put her hand up to his face and brought that same sexy mouth down to hers. The touch of it scalded her and she parted her lips almost instantly, letting the sensual heat of his tongue invade her. The taste of him brought an avalanche of passionate memories and she willingly gave herself up to the eroticism of them. No other man tasted like Mac. Not that she'd had vast experience, or *any* other experience for that matter—Mac had been her one and only lover—but she couldn't imagine any other man setting her alight so completely. Sex on legs, she had mused in fright when her gaze had collided with his that first time on the tube—and her instincts had all been right.

Behind her back his hand slid down further to caress

her shapely bottom. Naked, that particular part of her anatomy felt like velvet, he remembered. Deepening the kiss, he urged her hips flush against him, parting her thighs with his knee, his sex hardening to the point of pain.

'Did you make love to Amelie or was it just sex?'

The question was like being stripped naked and dunked into a pool of freezing ice. His heart pounding, Mac let Tara go then stepped back, his face a barely controlled mask of raw fury.

'You really know how to kill a mood, don't you? You do that to all the men in your life or is that particular torture reserved purely for me?'

Pained, Tara tunnelled her fingers through her hair and looked at him aghast. 'There haven't been any other men in my life since you—' Choked, she broke off, trying desperately to reassemble her tumbled defences. The question about his ex-girlfriend had come out of nowhere, taking her by surprise—but she must have wanted to ask it or it wouldn't have been in her consciousness. Now she couldn't help wondering. What had this Amelie been like? Had she been shattered when things hadn't worked out with Mac? The way Tara had been shattered when he'd left?

Even though he was furious with her, Mac felt gratified by her answer. He didn't quite know how he would have coped with the idea that she'd slept with other men—even though she had every right under the circumstances.

'She lived with me for six months. We were intimate sporadically at best, at worst—hardly at all. Amelie was a very fastidious woman—she didn't exactly like to get herself in a sweat, if you know what I mean?'

Tara did…only too clearly. His base reference made

her hot all over and she cursed herself for breaking the mood. What had she been thinking of?

'I'm sorry... I had to ask.'

'Sorry that my love life wasn't all it could have been or sorry that she didn't enjoy it?'

Her cheeks flamed red. Suddenly she felt as if a million flashing cameras were trained on her. She could barely bring herself to meet his glance.

'You're angry.'

'Yeah, I'm angry. Go the top of the class!' His response was like whiplash. 'You have every right to feel aggrieved by what I did to you, Tara, but you don't have to try and emasculate me to make a point. The fire's burning low. I'll wait until it's nearly out then I'm going to turn in. In the meantime, I think I need something a little stronger than this.' Striding away from her, he took his untouched drink out into the kitchen, leaving Tara standing there wishing she could roll back time to the moment before she had so thoughtlessly blurted out her crass question about his ex.

She wanted him. The need was a physical ache that had her twisting and writhing in the big double bed where she slept. Powerful erotic dreams of Mac had tormented her for hours, making her more than just a little hot and bothered. Pushing back the bunched-up patchwork quilt, she swung her long legs to the floor, dragging her hands feverishly through her hair as she stared at the grey, misty dawn that was seeping through her half-drawn curtains. Reaching for her silky aquamarine robe, she pulled it on then padded barefoot into the corridor. Somewhere a clock ticked and at the end of the hallway glowed a soft red light in front of a portrait of Jesus Christ—the famous 'Sacred Heart' that Beth had once told her shone in practically every home in Ireland.

Taking a deep, shuddering breath, Tara tried to remember which room was Mac's. There were four doors down the corridor including her own, two on the left and two on the right. Gathering her courage in both hands, she peeked into three of them, her heart in her mouth when Mac was not to be found anywhere.

Had he been so mad at her that he'd decided to fly back to the UK without her? He wouldn't do that... would he? Momentarily paralysed by fear and self-doubt, she gave herself a little shake then walked slowly into the living room. She came to an immediate standstill when she saw his long, muscular physique draped awkwardly along the couch. He'd obviously fetched a counterpane from his room and some time in the night it had covered him, but now it lay in a colourful heap on the floor in front of him. Tara shivered violently and not just from the chill in the room. Soft-footed, she moved towards him.

He was still wearing his sweater and jeans. Gazing down at his handsome sleeping face, his light hair swept back from his forehead, she studied the faint little ridges on his brow and the new lines beside his eyes. It made her hurt inside to think of him working so hard and so long without a break and she wished—not for the first time—that he wouldn't drive himself so hard. The man needed to cut himself a little slack. He had a successful, thriving business—he didn't have to prove anything to anyone. Least of all her... All she had ever been of his hard work and ambition was intolerant. Funny how she could see that so clearly now, as if someone had switched on a light bulb in her brain.

Hands shaking a little, she clutched at the silky material of her robe as if to prevent herself from reaching out to touch him. But oh, how she wanted to touch him. The need was consuming her. She might be cold on the outside but inside she was burning up.

Finally, her pulse racing wildly, she reached out and laid her hand on his chest. Mac opened his eyes. Without a word his fingers curled around the fine bones of her wrist and tugged her towards him. Losing her balance, Tara tumbled on top of him, her breath shooting out of her in a shocked little whoosh. Then he was kissing her, making love to her with his mouth while his hands roamed her body, stroking, pressing, caressing, until she was too weak to fight the matching need that throbbed through her and surrendered instead to the powerful conflagration that was consuming them both. She drew back momentarily to look at him, her hair softly dishevelled, shimmering green eyes glazed with desire, and when he protested Tara placed her finger across his lips as if silently begging him not to speak, just to feel. Dropping his head back onto the tasselled cushion behind him, Mac held his breath as her hands moved down to his pelvis, stroked across the hard, aching ridge behind his fly, then slowly eased down his zipper. He groaned and would have reached for her again but she was working his jeans down to his knees and then doing the same with his black silk boxers. Heat slammed into Mac like a force of nature. His mouth went dry as she straddled him with her long, pale thighs and slowly but deftly took him inside herself. Deeper and deeper she took him, and as she began to rock herself gently back and forth Mac seriously thought her scorching heat would set him on fire. Then she bent towards him and kissed him and Mac reached for her, his hands stroking across the rigid, velvet tips of her breasts through her thin nightshirt, squeezing and cupping. When she sat back to give him greater access, he covered them hungrily with his mouth so that she cried out, releasing his name in soft, breathy little gasps that had all the nerve endings on the surface of his hot, awakened skin exploding with pleasure.

Memories Tara had held in her heart came flooding back. *Arousing* memories. There wasn't a surface in their apartment that they hadn't made love on at one time or another. They'd always been so hungry for one another—as if they could never get enough. Bringing her concentration firmly back to the present, Tara sighed, fierce pleasure shuddering through her like an electrical current on high voltage—she could practically hear it hum. With every rocking movement of her pelvis, Mac thrust into her more deeply, until finally the intensity of the pleasure became just too much to bear. Exquisite little sensations of heat erupted inside her, eliciting a ragged cry from her soul as her soft, moist walls clasped and unclasped his hardness in a primal rhythm all of their own, until she felt his own powerful capitulation as he bucked against her. Breathing hard, he held her hips firm beneath his hands—right where he wanted her—before slowly letting her go. When he opened his gorgeous blue eyes, his lips parting in a devastating smile that made Tara feel as if she was drowning in moonlight and passion, she dared to smile back, her heartbeat wild in her chest.

'I remembered that's how you like to be woken up.' Her voice was unconsciously silky.

'Ten out of ten for effort, Mrs Simmonsen,' he responded huskily, knowing that calling her that made him believe she belonged to him and him alone—or would do again soon if there was any real justice in the world. To his absolute delight she blushed like a schoolgirl and the blood in Mac's veins heated and throbbed anew. In an instant he wanted her again. When she would have moved away, he stilled her with his hands, pulling her back down, his eyes darkening as desire stirred once again in his loins.

Tara bit her lip in shock but obediently stayed where she was, allowing Mac to push her robe off her shoulders, then to slowly and deliberately unbutton her nightshirt until she was naked before him.

'You're so beautiful, baby.' His voice was hoarse with admiration as he skimmed his fingers round her perfect, sexy little navel then proceeded to do the same to her breasts. 'And if you think you're running away from me any time soon…think again, because I have plans for you.'

'Plans?' Her pulse skittered as she stared down into his melting blue gaze.

'Yes, plans,' he teased. 'And they may just keep us both here all morning.' Removing his sweater, his broad, magnificent shoulders and flat, hard stomach exposed to her hungry gaze, Mac deftly swapped places so that Tara ended up flat on her back beneath him, her blonde hair a bright, silky mass on the red tasselled cushion behind her head. Mac sucked in a deep, satisfying breath. 'Now I've got you right where I want you and, barring an earthquake or other acts of God, that's where you're staying until I've proven to you we're making love and not just having sex. Is that understood?'

Sliding her hand round his back, loving the feel of those strong, rippling muscles slick beneath her fingers,

Tara managed a briefly tremulous smile. 'Do I look as if I'm about to run away?' she asked.

Later, Tara walked down to the beach. She'd left Mac reading a recipe book of all things—one of many lining the bookshelf in the kitchen—surprised and intrigued when he insisted he was going to rustle something up for lunch. Wrapping her arms tightly round the oversize chunky-knit sweater she wore—one of Mac's that she'd borrowed—she sniffed at the sexy masculine fragrance emanating from the material and shivered with pleasure. There wasn't a single place on her body that hadn't received her husband's passionate and loving ministrations and she had the aftershocks to prove it. Her limbs had the consistency of semolina and her breasts throbbed from the insatiable demands of his mouth. It had been a long time since her body had been so thoroughly loved. Mac was right: the conflagration they'd ignited between them hadn't just been about sex—they had really and truly made love. Even if he hadn't exactly professed to love her.

Turning her head, Tara gazed up at the house on the hill, her heart racing a little when she thought about living with Mac again. Had he meant it when he said they could look for a house in her home town? Would the quaint little market town be enough for her cosmopolitan, city-bred husband? Would he soon tire of the lack of urban culture? More to the point—would he soon tire of her?

And could she risk getting her heart broken all over again if he left? Even if she had announced to Beth that that was an impossibility because it was still broken from the last time.

A seagull squawked loudly overhead, stealing her

attention. Shading her eyes, Tara glanced skywards, feeling a deep longing that she couldn't begin to explain, except maybe to realise it was something about freedom. What was that saying? 'If you love somebody set them free.' Mac's devotion to his work had played a big part in their break-up but had Tara had the right to try and curtail his ambition? His passion? If she'd truly loved him she wouldn't have tried to restrain his desire to make his business a success. True, there'd been many times when he hadn't been there for her because he was needed at work, but equally she hadn't always been there for him when he wanted her to be. There'd been countless functions and dinners where she'd been invited to accompany her husband, including two black-tie events when Mac's company had won prestigious awards, yet Tara had refused to go with him, preferring to sulk in their apartment alone, feeling hard-done-by and aggrieved. And Mac hadn't even given her a hard time about it.

She dropped her gaze to stare down at the matchless white sand beneath her feet. A strong sea breeze gusted in, tossing her hair. Pushing it out of her eyes, she reflected that right now she was confused about a lot of things. All she could do was just take one small step at a time.

She twisted the plain platinum band on her finger. Whether this holiday together would lead to a more permanent arrangement she didn't know, but one thing she was sure of—her love for Mac hadn't diminished one jot since their break-up. It was the sole and only reason she hadn't sought him out for a divorce.

CHAPTER EIGHT

MAC was having a hard time staying awake and it wasn't just the heat from the fire that was making him drowsy. Years of sleep deprivation due to his work, nights when he'd burned the midnight oil well into the early hours poring over ad campaigns, trying to come up with some original idea that would blow the client away, plus the usual assortment of staff problems and headaches that came with running your own business—it all added up to a constant feeling of being below par. He was only just beginning to realise that he'd been running on empty for such a long time now that he almost believed that drained, tired feeling was normal.

Stifling another yawn, he stretched out his long jean-clad legs towards the fire, then put his hands behind his head and leaned back against the sofa. From somewhere in the house came the comforting strains of a tinkling piano. He didn't recognise the composer but he knew Tara was using the music as an accompaniment to her ballet exercises. His lips curved into a smile when he thought about how indignant she'd been when he asked if he could stay and watch. They both knew it wasn't a good idea. The fact that she was wearing tight black leggings and a skimpy little bodice thing that was like a second skin, and would be stretching her beautiful, supple body into all kinds of impossible positions to give those trained muscles of hers a workout, would simply be more temptation than Mac could take. But there wasn't anything to stop him imagining, was there? They'd whiled the whole morning away making love; 'making up for lost time,' as Mac had joked—and yet his body seemed to be in a permanent state of arousal whenever she was around. How he could have been so stupid as to believe that a woman like Amelie Duvall could come close to satisfying raw passion like his—passion that only someone like Tara could equal—he didn't know. If his father hadn't passed away so unexpectedly, and Mac had not had a kind of thirty-something panic about not having kids, nothing but nothing would have possessed him to suggest the possibility of marriage to such a woman. True, she'd impressed the hell out of his clients when they'd gone to dinner together, but then some of them had been just as superficial as Amelie herself—valuing status, careers, cars, houses, clothes more than they valued some of the more important things in life. Like a loving partner, a welcoming home and children. Things that Mac now craved with all his heart. Idly, he wondered if Tara would fall pregnant soon. He told himself the chances must be good since they'd both clearly abandoned the whole notion of using contraception.

When the telephone on the heavy oak sideboard purred suddenly into the silence, Mac stared at it in shock as if it were a ticking bomb. Uttering a few choice Anglo-Saxon phrases, he reluctantly got to his feet to answer it.

Glowing after her workout, her skin glistening with a thin sheen of perspiration and her muscles nicely aching, Tara popped her head into the living room on the way to her shower to suggest to Mac they open a bottle of wine when she returned. A fresh white towel thrown casually around her shoulders, she pushed open the door, only to hear his voice raised in conversation. It

took a few heart-stopping moments for her to realise
he was talking on the phone. He'd told her that no one
else knew he was here. Beneath the damp strands of
her fringe, Tara's brow creased into a frown. Perhaps
it was simply a wrong number? As she advanced further into the room, Mac turned at her entrance and the
slightly pained expression on his handsome features
confirmed that it was not.

For a moment after replacing the receiver, Mac said
nothing. He simply stood by the sideboard, rubbing the
back of his neck as if it was causing him pain. All the
muscles in Tara's stomach clenched with unease.

'Who was that?' she asked, her voice sounding too
loud in the big, silent room.

'Mitch Williams.'

'The chap who owns this house?'

'That's right.'

Then of course he would know that Mac was here—
would be familiar with the telephone number. Tara's
shoulders dropped with relief.

'Mitch is my second in command,' Mac continued,
'he—'

'You mean he works with you?' Immediately sus-
picious, Tara glared accusingly at her husband. 'It used
to be Graham Radlett…whatever happened to him?'

'Emigrated. To Spain.'

'Couldn't stand the pace, huh?'

'Something like that.'

'It's about work, isn't it? Do they want you to go
back?'

'There's a problem.' Unable to keep the strain from
his voice, Mac levelled his troubled blue eyes straight
at Tara, trying not to pay too much attention to the fact
that she looked tousled and gorgeous in her exercise

gear, the tight, stretchy clothing concealing nothing of the lithe, fit shape underneath.

'One of our biggest clients is screaming "lawsuit" unless I personally show up to placate him. If it were anything else I'd tell Mitch to handle it, I swear. All I need is an afternoon to meet him at his hotel... If I catch a flight in the morning I can be back by tomorrow night.'

'But we've only just got here!' Duelling with anger and disappointment at their holiday being interrupted as well as her newfound understanding of Mac's commitment to his job, Tara tugged the towel from around her neck and pressed it against her forehead.

'You'd better get on the phone to the airline, then,' she said airily, pretending a nonchalance she clearly didn't feel. *It wasn't fair!* she cried inside. Already she was missing him. Already work was sabotaging any chance they might have at a future together. 'I need a shower. Excuse me.'

'Tara, wait!'

Ignoring him, she hurried from the room.

Huddled into her ivory sheepskin jacket the following morning, Tara watched Mac collect his boarding pass from the airline desk, willing herself not to let her guard down. She was expecting to be disappointed, and her personal defence mechanism was kicking in big time. For all she knew he might be gone more than just a day as he so confidently assured her. For all she knew he might not come back at all.

'I've got ten minutes before I have to go to the boarding gate. Let's sit down.'

Tara could hardly bring herself to look at him as they sat—instead her gaze fluttered back and forth to the flickering television screens announcing flight departures.

'Tara.'

'What?' Giving him an impatient glance, she felt her heart turn over at those chiselled Scandinavian features of his, those direct cobalt-blue eyes that left her with nowhere to go. Why did she have to notice the long, lavish lashes that fringed those beautiful eyes at this stage in the game? Why did those powerful, broad shoulders beneath his black double-breasted jacket give her goose pimples just because they had inadvertently brushed against her as they sat?

'Everything's going to be all right. Trust me.'

'Is it?' Tears perilously close, Tara quickly averted her gaze. 'Do you think that someone up there doesn't like us?'

'I think that someone up there is giving us every chance to put things right.' Drawing her hand into his lap, he smiled. 'What happened to that famous optimism of yours?'

Her expression raw, Tara stared at him hard. 'I lost it the night you left. Didn't you know?'

It took Mac a moment or two to absorb the sudden pain in his chest. His fingers curled tightly around her small, pale hand. 'I didn't mean to hurt you. It was probably one of the worst decisions I've ever made. I know that now.'

'Just come back soon...please.' A single tear tracked down her face and she impatiently wiped it away lest anyone should see.

'That's something I'm only too happy to promise. I'll meet with the client, get things straightened out then jump on a plane back just as soon as I can. I've got Mitch's number so I'll ring you as soon as I know when. Will you come and meet me at the airport?'

She nodded as she pulled the hire-car keys out of her pocket, jangling them in front of him. 'You'll have to walk if I don't. Twenty-five miles in the dark—you might just make it back to the house by Christmas.'

He grinned and Tara felt the force of his smile like a physical blow to her solar plexus. God, the things that man could do to her with just a smile...

She spent most of the day around the house. Tuning in to the local radio for company, she listened with pleasure to an assortment of Irish chat and song, feeling somehow comforted by the famously lyrical notes of the voices and the music. Of course, Mac was on her mind most of the time but Tara tried to intersperse her desperate longing to see him with a whirl of activity and house-cleaning. Once she'd vacuumed every room, polished every surface and had the kitchen gleaming like the proverbial new pin, she turned her attentions to some cooking. Concocting her own improvised version of Irish stew, she left the huge pot simmering on the stove while she baked a batch of fruit scones. By the time her culinary pursuits were completed, the washing-up done and the kitchen floor swept for the second time that day, it was still only three in the afternoon and she still hadn't heard from Mac.

Moving across to the huge window in the living room, Tara stared edgily past the expanse of rolling green to the crystal-white waves lapping onto the shore in the distance. Folding her arms across her chest, she turned briefly to consider the silent telephone. Mind made up, she located her waterproof in the utility room, stuck her feet determinedly into her walking boots then made her way down to the beach. As soon as the fresh, gusty air hit her lungs, she felt the day's tension ease out of her body. She'd only be gone about an hour, she promised herself, her feet sinking slightly in the soft, impacted sand as she walked. Mac would be sure to ring by then.

But by eight o'clock that evening Tara still hadn't heard from him. Her heart heavy, she forced herself to eat a small bowl of the stew she'd made, then switched on the small television in a bid to distract herself from thoughts that dragged her along a road of gloom she didn't want to travel down. Finally, losing patience with the programme she had selected to watch—a very dull, too intellectual discussion on the arts—and weary of her own company, she picked up the phone and dialled her aunt's number back home.

'I was wondering when I'd hear from you,' Beth ventured cautiously after her niece had greeted her. 'How's it all going? You and Mac getting along all right?'

Recalling their morning of impromptu passion yesterday followed by more of the same last night, Tara couldn't help but blush profusely.

'We're getting along just fine, thank you very much. It's just the most beautiful country; so green it hurts your eyes. And the house we're in has the most amazing view of the sea.'

'I know, darling. Your grandparents came from County Cork, remember? I still have cousins in the village where they grew up. But, that aside, I'm really much more interested in you and Mac. I'm not sure how I feel about you being out there alone with him. Right now the jury is out as far as I'm concerned.'

Tara didn't see the point in adding to her aunt's concerns by sharing the news that Mac had had to rush back to London to see to business. She didn't pause to consider why she suddenly felt so protective of him either. Tucking her hair behind her ears, she sighed wistfully into the receiver.

'You were the one who said we needed to talk, remember? Well, we're talking.' Amongst other things.

'So what exactly are you talking about? Does the subject of divorce still feature in the frame?'

'You would have made a good recruit to the Gestapo, you know that?'

'Darling, the fact that you're being so close-mouthed about the whole thing makes me think you're still confused. Don't let Mac railroad you into making any decisions you're not ready for, you hear me?'

'I hear you, Aunt.' Tara rolled her eyes heavenwards.

'And don't call me "Aunt" like that. It makes me feel like some crusty old thing well past her sell-by date!'

'When are you going to get it through your thick head that you're not old!' Smiling affectionately, Tara turned her attention to the still flickering television screen, where the tedious discussion she'd grown impatient with was coming to a thankful close. Feeling increasingly on edge in case Mac was trying to get through to her, she was suddenly anxious to bring the call to an end. 'Anyway, I've got to go now; I only wanted a brief chat and I think I can hear Mac calling,' she fibbed, crossing her fingers.

'Well, ring me as soon as you know when you're coming home. I miss not having you around.'

'If you need company, why don't you ask Peter Trent over the road to come over for coffee? I know he has a soft spot for you and you might just find you have more in common than you think.'

'Antique books and antique furniture—we'd make a great pair, wouldn't we? Darling, when I get that desperate it'll be time for me to go into a home! Anyway, give me your number just in case I feel like a chat.'

Willingly, Tara did so.

'Take care, now,' her aunt instructed, 'speak soon…and if you're in the area don't forget to kiss the blarney stone for me!'

Two hours later there'd been no phone call from Mac and Tara had to resign herself to the stark fact that there probably wasn't going to be. Not tonight, anyway. Her emotions veering from anger to desperation, she switched off all the lamps in the living room and glumly made her way to bed.

Was she a fool to trust him again after he had let her down so badly? It was the last thought she forlornly remembered thinking before her eyelids drooped helplessly and she fell off into a deep, troubled sleep.

Never again! Never again would Mac put himself through such hoops for the sake of smoothing a petulant rich client's ruffled feathers—no matter how important that particular client deemed himself. He was only glad that at the end of an aggravating, completely tiresome day—apart from the fact that he'd managed to rescue the account and avert a lawsuit—he was now back at the house where he should have been all along with Tara. At least he'd had the gratification of telling his client that next time he should take his business elsewhere because Mac really couldn't be doing with the hassle. To his surprise, his client had quickly back-pedalled, assuring him he wouldn't even consider using another agency because he had always been very satisfied in the past.

Seeing the loquacious cab-driver off with a more than generous tip, Mac lifted the small navy-blue holdall he had taken with him then wearily climbed the steps to the house. All the lights were off save for the porch light and, searching for the spare house key—which Mitch had assured him would be under the mat outside the door—Mac quietly let himself inside.

Anxious to return, he hadn't bothered to telephone Tara first. Besides, it was just after three in the morning and he hadn't wanted to wake her. Most of all he hadn't wanted her to make that long, lonely drive to the airport in the dark to meet him. Getting a cab had been the most sensible move, after all.

Dropping his jacket onto a hall chair, Mac left his bag there too, then, kicking off his shoes, made his way along the long, dim corridor to Tara's bedroom. The heavy drapes in her room hadn't been drawn and moonlight drifted in, making everything in the room appear in soft focus. She was lying on her front, her long, slim arms stretched out on the plump white pillow beneath her head. Mac felt a hitch in his heart at the sight of all that tousled blonde hair.

Bending down to her level on the bed, he brushed back her hair, feeling the warm, whispery softness of her breath trail across his wrist. He didn't intend to wake her, only indulge himself in the sight of her for a little while. Although he'd only been gone less than twenty-four hours, he'd had plenty of time to miss her.

'Mac?' Stirring, she turned over then wriggled into a semi-sitting position—sleepy green eyes squinting then focusing on his face.

'I'm back, sweetheart.'

'You bastard!'

For a moment Mac was so taken aback by the blow to his shoulder that he didn't bother to defend himself. But when Tara aimed another blow, then another, he grabbed her wrists to deflect any further attack, then stared in stunned bewilderment at her angry, flushed face. 'What the hell was that for?' he demanded, furious.

'You lied to me!'

'I didn't lie to you, I—'

'It doesn't matter how you dress it up, Mac. You didn't even have the courtesy to ring me and let me know you'd be late!' She yanked at her wrists but Mac held on to them with fingers of steel, his expression grim.

'Listen to me! The meeting took longer than I thought and the client was a couple of hours late. I had to wine and dine the guy then put him in a cab home. By the time I did all that, caught up with Mitch then rang the airline to book a flight back, it was getting on for nine in the evening. The earliest flight I could get on wasn't till after midnight. I didn't ring you because I didn't want you driving out to the airport late at night to meet me. I thought it would be easier to just jump in a cab and arrive...sort of surprise you,' he added wryly, thinking that he'd certainly achieved that—but not in the way he'd intended. The unwanted realisation that he had become just a little *too* absorbed in his work sent a wave of guilt eddying through him and he shoved it impatiently away to the back of his mind.

Still struggling against his iron-like hold on her wrists, Tara pouted angrily, her pulse racing. 'It's just like old times, isn't it, Mac? You make me a promise then you don't keep it. Nothing's changed.'

The despondency in her voice completely undid him. Warring with the rage he felt at being misunderstood when he was only doing what he thought was right, as well as being desperate to hold her, Mac swore softly beneath his breath and released her.

'*Everything's* changed, Tara. Despite what you think, I no longer put my work first. This was a unique situation that needed my expertise to sort it out. Whether you like it or not, I still have a responsibility to the people who work for me. Their jobs are dependent on my agency being a success. I couldn't just leave them in the lurch.'

'No. That's not something you'd ever do, Mac.' A wave of shame washed over her as she rubbed at her throbbing wrists. Her fears had run away with her. When Mac hadn't telephoned earlier she'd assumed the worst. She'd assumed that she wasn't important enough for him to want to fly back at the earliest opportunity to be with her. Now she heard the frustration and pain in his voice as he'd explained what had happened and she felt chastised because she knew he was a man of integrity who wouldn't knowingly let people down if he could help it. That included her.

'I'm sorry.'

'There's nothing to be sorry for. I'm the one who should apologise. Next time I'll make sure I ring you first.' Rising to his feet, he rubbed a hand across his eyes and Tara felt a pang at the sudden weariness etched into those incredibly handsome features. 'Go back to sleep. Goodnight, Tara.'

Panicked, she pushed a shaky hand through her hair. 'Where are you going?'

His gaze seemed worryingly distant. 'To bed. I'm practically dead on my feet.'

'Don't you want a drink? Something to eat?' She swung her legs to the floor and stood up. She was wearing a plain pink nightie with shoestring straps that didn't come close to disguising the delectable curves beneath it.

As attracted as he was, plain fatigue still got the better of Mac. 'I'm fine,' he shrugged. 'I had a sandwich and some coffee earlier. All I want now is my bed.'

A brief smile that was more like a grimace on his lips, he left Tara standing there, closing the door firmly shut behind him.

When she walked into the kitchen the next morning there was no sign of him. Instead she found a note propped up against a milk jug on the table. It told her he'd gone for a walk on the beach and to go ahead and have breakfast without him.

The thought of food made her stomach roil. How could she eat when her whole system was in turmoil? Chewing down heavily on her lip, Tara hurried into the utility room, grabbed her waterproof and ran out of the house to make her way down to the beach.

She found him skimming pebbles into the sea. 'You've got to learn to trust me, Tara. This isn't going to work otherwise.' After a brief glance her way, he continued to skim stones.

Swallowing hard, she jammed her hands into the big patch pockets of her jacket. Last night she'd been distraught at the idea of losing him again. When he hadn't telephoned to say when he would be back, she'd been frantic with worry. All manner of crazy thoughts had flown through her mind; including what if the plane crashed and he was killed before she'd had the chance to tell him that she loved him? Had always loved him—even when they were apart? That was why her reaction, when he finally showed up, had been so wild.

'Trust is a big leap for me,' she confessed quietly.

'I know.' Wiping his hands down the front of his jeans, Mac closed the gap between them, considering her slowly with a long, heated glance that made her toes tingle nicely in her boots. 'That's why I'm giving you all the time in the world to make it. Right now all I want to do is be with you. I'm in this for the long haul, Tara. I'll do whatever I have to do to gain your trust. That's a promise.'

Something settled inside her. Something light and good, like someone shining a torch in pitch-black darkness. Without a word she moved into his arms, savouring the sharp, cold scent of the sea that clung to him and mingled with the warm, indefinable essence of the man himself. Burying her face in the thick, soft wool of his sweater, she breathed him in like oxygen, drank him in like wine.

'Are you hungry?' Green eyes bright, she regarded him with a teasing, happy expression on her face.

'For you...not for food,' Mac replied, his voice rough with need, his hands settling possessively on her hips.

'Well, maybe I can tempt you with a little of both?' She slid her palms up his chest as he angled his head towards her for a kiss then playfully pushed him away and started to run down the beach. 'But you've got to catch me first! Think you can do it?'

Mac grinned wolfishly. 'Sweetheart, with you as the prize I could take on the whole British Olympic relay team and win!'

Moving into a long-legged sprint, he charged after

her, closing the gap between them even more quickly than he'd expected. When Tara turned to gauge his progress and saw him gaining on her, she took a fit of the giggles and ground to a halt, holding her side where a stitch had begun.

'Wow!' Her eyes were shining when he drew up alongside her. 'You must have been in training. That was impressive!'

'Not half as impressive as I'm going to be in the bedroom, Mrs Simmonsen.'

Jaw determined, Mac swept her up into his arms, experiencing the inevitable blood rush to his loins when she slid her arms happily around him and teased, 'Promises, promises.'

'What? You think I can't rise to the challenge?'

Ignoring the innuendo, Tara couldn't help but sigh as she gazed into his resolutely handsome face. 'I think you can rise to any damn thing you put your mind to, Mac...I really do.'

CHAPTER NINE

AFTER they'd been driving for some time, Mac stopped the car in a breathtaking area composed of desolate rocky plateaux beneath a sharp blue sky with the chill of winter in it, known locally as the Burren. After considering the view for several long, satisfying seconds he turned abruptly to Tara. 'OK, give me the map.'

'No! I can read it.'

'Be a good girl and give me the map, Tara.'

'I said no! And please don't patronise me in that oh-so-reasonable tone of voice you obviously reserve for air-head secretaries! I know what I'm doing. I've been reading maps since I was a child.'

'Then can you explain to me why we're lost?' His mouth nudging into a smile, Mac would never have believed himself capable of this much patience in any driving situation—but the fact of the matter was, Tara was so damned determined to take charge of their little outing that all he could do was sit back in admiration and enjoy himself. Being lost simply added to the flavour.

Irritated that she couldn't seem to locate on the map exactly where they were in relation to where they were headed, Tara scratched her head then glared at the big, handsome man beside her. 'I'd hate to work for you, you know that?'

'*I'd* hate you to work for me too.'

When her forehead creased into a hurt little frown Mac laughed, stroking his finger down her cheek.

'You'd be a constant distraction. I'd never get anything done.'

Mellowing, Tara leaned towards him, sliding her hand deliberately along a hard-muscled thigh encased in dark blue denim. 'Would that be a good thing or a bad thing, do you think?'

'I think…' he dropped several little kisses on her softly parted lips, each one engendering the explosive heat of a small landmine '…that right now you'd better reserve all your employable skills to reading that map and getting us out of here…before I have to resort to the first rule of survival when lost in unknown terrain.'

'Oh?' Her breath quickening beneath the hot, drugging kisses that were becoming increasingly more demanding at every touch, Tara's aroused green gaze regarded Mac in tremulous anticipation. 'What's that, then?'

'Check for injuries,' he said huskily as his hand slipped under her sweater and found the soft, womanly swell of her breast beneath her bra.

'But…neither of us is injured.'

'Don't teeth-marks count?' With a low growl, Mac pulled away from her mouth, dragging his teeth along the side of her neck. She felt the sharp pleasure-pain when he nipped the sensitive flesh, his fingers squeezing her nipple at the same time. Her blood sang in her veins. She slid her hand along his jawline, luxuriating in her ability to just reach out and touch, to savour, to sample his honed, hard flesh when for five long years she'd been denied such hungry pleasures. How had she lived without him all that time, let alone breathed? Emotion jammed in her throat and for several staggering moments Tara was blinded by hot, stinging tears. The intensity of her feelings, her overwhelming love for this driven, hard-working, single-minded, beautiful man, whose baby she had borne and lost without his even knowing—it all came at her like a huge wave, engulfing her without mercy.

Mac knew the very moment when her mind was on something else, something other than this white-hot electric heat they were generating between them as easily as looking at each other. Regretfully he moved his hand from the silky touch of her breast then eased down her sweater. Then he removed her far enough away from him to register the shimmering evidence of tears in her beautiful green eyes. His gut clenched. It devastated him to see her cry.

'What's all this about, hmm?' Tilting her chin, he eased the pad of his thumb back and forth across her delicate jaw.

'I'm sorry I didn't tell you about the baby, Mac. Sorry I believed you wouldn't care. Can you ever forgive me?'

Swallowing with difficulty at the mention of their son, Mac took a second or two to compose himself. In his heart he was honestly working on coming to terms with their loss, easing it by vowing that if their union was blessed with other children he would be there every step of the way. Tara would never have any cause to doubt his commitment again...not in this life.

'Of course I forgive you. We both made mistakes. I don't think either one of us set out to deliberately hurt the other. A lot of water has gone under the bridge, Tara; we can't get back what we had, but we can start anew.'

'I still don't know, Mac.' Linking her hands with his, she managed an endearingly lopsided little smile. 'What I want, I mean. I mean, I want you but...' I'm terrified, she acknowledged silently, terrified it will all go wrong, terrified that I won't be able to bear the pain if you walk out again...

'It's all right, baby. You don't have to make any decisions right now. We'll just take one day at a time and see how it goes.' It killed him to put on such a show of calm when inside his heart felt as if it was going to climb out of his chest. Some way, somehow, he was going to win her back or die in the attempt. Planting a sizzling little kiss on her upturned mouth, Mac sat back a little to enjoy the effect—dewy eyes, rosy cheeks and moist lips, not to mention tremulously rising and falling milk-white breasts in her V-necked sweater. Her response did wonders for his confidence—not to mention his libido.

'If you consider the fact that I've hardly been able to keep my hands off you since we came on this little holiday and you haven't banished me to the nearest dungeon yet, I'd say we had a pretty good chance of making a go of things, wouldn't you?'

Lifting her shoulders, Tara sighed. The man was pretty damn irresistible and the fact of the matter was she really didn't want to resist him at all. Suddenly embarrassed by his searching gaze, she made a big fuss of straightening out the much perused map, then, squinting down, prodded it triumphantly with her finger. 'I found it! We passed that place five minutes ago. I reckon we must be just a couple of miles away from the caves. If we drive along this road a little bit further, it's bound to be signposted.'

Feigning disappointment, Mac yawned and stretched. 'You mean I've got to start driving again?'

Squirming beneath that lazily hot look that had her wriggling in her seat, Tara diverted her attention to the stunning views all around them. 'Of course you've got to start driving! There's a lot to see. And after we've visited the Ailwee caves I want to go and see the Cliffs of Moher—it's supposed to be the most spectacular sight and I've got loads of film in the camera I want to use up.'

'And after that?' he asked, hands curving round the steering wheel in a way that made Tara wish they were on her body.

'And after that...' There was a slight hitch in her breathing as she stole a greedy glance, silently acknowledging that if they were in bed together right now it would be seriously wild—clawing at the sheets, holding on to the bedpost wild... Clearing her throat, she gazed deliberately ahead. 'We'll find something to keep us both out of mischief.'

As he switched on the ignition, a sweep of heat coloured Mac's jaw. 'God, I love it when you talk dirty,' he said hoarsely and the car lurched a little as it started to move.

Standing on a narrow iron bridge with a dizzying drop below, Tara clung on to Mac's arm, daring herself to look down as their cheerful Irish guide knowledgeably explained the difference between stalagmites and stalactites. The two-million-year-old caves were darkly spectacular and the dimly lit interior and the dense, dank smell that arose from the ancient rocks seemed to transport them into a world underground that was hard to imagine even existed when you were walking on terra firma outside.

'Isn't this amazing?' Mac whispered as they moved off slowly behind the single line of tourists following the guide.

'There's one thing about me you might need a little

reminder of,' Tara whispered back, keeping a firm hold on the muscular arm beneath his soft suede jacket.

'What's that?'

'I'm not very good with heights. I get vertigo just going up a couple of rungs on a ladder.'

He chuckled, the deeply sensuous sound making her tingle. 'Now you mention it, I do recall you refusing to go up in the glass elevator at Lloyd's when we were invited for cocktails one time. Remember?'

'I remember being thankful I already had such well-developed calf muscles because walking up all those stairs was like hiking up K2!'

Fifteen minutes later, after the guide had dutifully warned them, the cave was plunged into absolute darkness, to demonstrate the inky blackness of the caves without light—a condition that their discoverer had had to contend with. Tara was glad of Mac's warm fingers linking reassuringly with hers, because being in the dark was another phobia that plagued her.

Beside her, he moved in closer, his free hand cupping her cheek. 'You OK? I know you don't like the dark.'

'Brave, aren't I?' Tara replied with a self-deprecating little shrug.

'Bravest woman I know,' Mac whispered next to her ear, and was it her imagination or did he just drop the briefest of kisses on her sensitive lobe? A butterfly's wing couldn't have been softer—or felt more delicious.

Her insides were zinging with joy—not to mention lust. If they didn't get out of here soon and into the daylight she wouldn't be walking straight! Feeling relieved when the light came back on, illuminating all the dark corners where water trickled down, transforming the caves into some kind of magical fairy grotto,

Tara smiled up at Mac. She was suddenly thrilled at the idea that they were getting to know each other all over again—like new lovers anticipating each other's next little touch or smile and longing for it—and wondered if he felt like that too.

'Penny for them.' Squeezing her hand, Mac led the way as they trailed more slowly behind the chatting line of tourists towards the exit.

'I'm feeling good,' she confessed, astonished to find that she really meant it.

'Me too.' He stopped to touch the tip of her nose, grinning. 'Now, let's play tourist and go raid the souvenir shop.'

From an array of soft toys of all shapes and sizes, he bought her a charming black cat with emerald eyes and ribbon to match, as well as an oversized T-shirt with an advertising slogan emblazoned on the front, which, he boldly stated in front of the smiling assistant, she could wear in bed.

In turn, Tara purchased a beautiful hardbacked book full of glossy colour photographs of the county, presenting it to Mac when they were back in the car ready to make their way to the majestic Cliffs of Moher.

Visibly moved, he turned it over in his hands, carefully separating the pages to interestedly study the pictures. 'Will you sign it for me?' Taking an expensive-looking gold fountain pen out of his inside jacket pocket, he handed it to her along with the book.

'Sure.' Suddenly embarrassed, Tara opened the front page and wrote with a slightly shaky hand:

'Mac—thanks for a wonderful day. Love, Tara.'

Automatically about to add several 'x's to represent kisses, she stopped herself just in time, blushed, closed the book then returned it and the pen to Mac.

'Thank you.'

'You're welcome.' She stared straight ahead, not trusting herself to look at him right then because it was taking all her self-control not to throw herself into his arms.

'Want to go home?'

'Why?' Her head spun round, and she was shocked to see the raw desire in slumberous blue eyes that were consuming her whole, inch by inch.

'Do you really need to ask?'

'But what about the Cliffs of Moher?'

To Tara's surprise he threw back his head and laughed out loud. 'Sweetheart, they've been around for thousands of years—I think they'll still be around tomorrow or the next day if we want to come back then.'

Embarrassed colour made her cheeks burn. 'Very funny. I'm glad you—' But her words stopped midstream when Mac suddenly threw open the car door and hurried across the tarmac towards a little toddling child wandering across the car park. The child was clearly distressed and, gathering him up in his arms, Mac held the toddler concernedly to his chest, talking to him, offering comfort. Tara's heart stalled. Life was so unfair. He clearly would have made the most wonderful father. Maybe he still *would*. She was out of the car in less than a minute, heart racing at the thought, her mouth curving in a sympathetic smile as the child's distraught mother reached Mac and threw her arms around him and the child.

'I was in the gift shop,' she was crying, 'I only let go of his hand for just a second. Oh, my God! What can I say? Thank you, thank you.' Hugging the child to her, she pulled him deep into her chest, directing a wobbly smile at Mac. 'Bless you. I don't know what I would have done if he'd wandered off and got lost—'

'It's OK.' Mac squeezed the woman's arm reassuringly then ruffled the toddler's curly blond hair. 'He's all right now. He probably just wanted to go exploring and didn't even realise he'd lost you until a minute ago. Look, he's smiling.' And he was. The child turned his head to beam at Mac as though he'd known him all his life. Tara drew level, her smile still in place. Mac took one look at her and hauled her hard against his chest.

'My wife,' he told the woman with the child, making no effort to conceal the pride and possession he clearly felt.

'Pleased to meet you. Do you have children yourselves?'

'No.' Tara heard the heavy throb of Mac's heartbeat next to her ear as he answered gravel-voiced, felt his torso stiffen as if to fend off a blow. 'No, we don't have children.'

Lifting her head, Tara held Mac's suddenly tortured gaze. 'But we're hoping to,' she said clearly, 'very soon.'

'They change your life for ever but you wouldn't be without them.' The woman fussed over her small son, her relieved smile breaking free like sunshine.

'So I've heard.' His hand reaching for hers, Mac pulled Tara to his side as if eager to be going, the expression on his face now full of hope and need and longing that he couldn't hide.

'Well, good luck to you both. You make a lovely couple... I'm sure you'll be wonderful parents too. Come on, Michael, let's see if Mummy can find you a nice sweetie in the shop.'

'Take care!' Tara called after the woman as she left.

'Home?' Mac suggested beside her.

'Home,' she agreed, tugging him urgently in the direction of their car.

They didn't make it to the bedroom. The distance from the front door to the nearest available bed was just too far. During the long drive home the tension between them had built and built and they'd hardly spoken a word to each other because the slightest, most infinitesimal thing could so easily tip the balance between civility and sheer animal need. Tara squealed when Mac slammed the door behind them then pushed her up against the entrance wall, his expression almost brutal with want. All pretence at restraint gone, his hard, hungry kiss knocked her for six. Reeling from the clash of teeth and tongues, intoxicated by the seductive masculine taste of his clever, mobile mouth, Tara melted into the wall as he unzipped her jeans, wrenched them down to her knees then wordlessly helped her out of them. Even as she kicked off her shoes, he had both hands on her hips, giving the same rough treatment to her underwear, yanking down her panties to her feet then parting her thighs—plunging into her wetness with his fingers before claiming her lips in another primal, passionate kiss that made her blood roar and her thoughts tumble crazily.

'Oh, God…Mac.' Blindly her hands reached for the zipper on his jeans; she was weak with want, she couldn't wait much longer, she couldn't wait even a second more before—

Releasing himself into her hands, he let her caress him briefly before guiding himself surely and expertly inside her. Everything clenched at that first deep thrust of possession and she was barely aware of his hands lifting her buttocks to position himself more deeply. 'I think I've dreamt of this every night since we've been apart,' he breathed raggedly against her mouth, blue eyes dark as midnight. 'Tell me...tell me what you want and you can have it...anything.'

Threading her fingers through the thick blond strands of his hair, Tara closed her eyes, gasping as Mac plunged again and again, deeper, harder, until she lost all sense of time and space and who she was. Nothing else seemed to matter. Passion transported her to a whole other world and all she could do was yield to the most profoundly intense pleasure she'd ever experienced in her life.

'You, Mac. I want *you*...all of you. Don't stop, please don't stop or I'll die.' In answer, he shoved up her sweater, released both breasts from her bra, then took one of them deep into his mouth. Her hips bucked against his as wave after wave of deep, swirling gratification swept over her, leaving her body shaking, her mind suspended in a place where thoughts and intentions and past hurts had no consequence. As she sank against the hard-muscled strength of his chest, she almost felt Mac swell inside her. She registered the tangible tension in his body just a split-second before he spilled himself into her most feminine core with a grated groan, resting his head momentarily between her breasts while he recovered himself. Their loving had been hot, hard and fast...just the way she'd so wantonly craved it.

When he eased her back down, tipping her chin towards him so that he could fasten his gaze on her eyes, he delivered the sexiest, most smouldering smile known to woman and almost brought Tara to her knees with the power of it.

'You may well smile,' she said quietly, her voice scratchy. 'You were a very naughty boy.'

Sliding his fingers between her legs, making her gasp out loud with the audacity of it, Mac grinned roguishly with the stunning confidence of a virile male who knew he could supply whatever his woman wanted—and then some. 'Want me to do it again?' he asked.

Propped up on one elbow, his free hand drifting lazily up and down Tara's naked spine, Mac wondered how long it would take her to wake. The hours after midnight had not seen much sleeping. Although he was tired his body was still restless and thrumming from their lovemaking, and God help him but he wanted more. No matter how often his body mated with hers, it never seemed to be enough. For three days now they'd been in and out of bed—only deviating to eat and shower and maybe walk on the beach—and if lovemaking were an Olympic sport they'd surely be lead contenders. Had it always been this intense between them? This good? Or had the time they'd been apart merely intensified the need? His heart throbbed a little when Tara mumbled something into her pillow and turned her head to gaze sleepily up at him.

His hand slipped lower down her spine to rest possessively on the undulating curve of her bottom. 'What did you say?'

She pushed her softly tousled blonde fringe out of her eyes, her expression drowsily concerned. 'I asked if you'd been to sleep at all?'

'Not so that you'd notice.' Grinning, Mac let his fingers drift onto the backs of her thighs beneath the cool white sheet, making deliberate and delicious little inroads to the softer flesh between them.

'Ma-a-a-c.' Groaning out loud, she rolled abruptly onto her back, taking most of the sheet with her.

'What?'

'I'm determined to get outside and get some exercise today, that's what. You're turning me into a thoroughly decadent and lazy woman!' Wriggling into a sitting position, she yanked the sheet further up to cover her breasts and bit her lip to stop herself from laughing out loud when Mac tried to relieve her of it.

'Just one kiss,' he pleaded huskily, blue eyes crinkling at the corners, 'one little kiss and I'll let you go...if that's what you want.'

They both knew it wouldn't stop at 'one little kiss.' Already Tara's body was tingling with anticipation, the place between her thighs throbbing and damp with need, her lush mouth swollen from the hundreds of kisses she'd received the night before...

God, he was wonderful. Her heart swelled with love for him. Spending time together, free from the demands and considerations of their normal lives, Tara had discovered a whole new side to Mac—or at least one she'd almost forgotten existed. He was playful and loving, tender and passionate, considerate and strong—all the qualities that would surely break the resolve of even the world's most resilient woman.

'All right, then,' she said, teasing, one hand reaching out to push the sexy lock of gold hair away from his forehead. 'I'll let you have one kiss—only if you promise to cook me breakfast.'

Blue eyes going dark, Mac tugged at the sheet to expose the beautiful, creamy fullness of her naked breasts. 'It's a deal.'

'And I'm not talking cornflakes and a piece of toast here, Mac Simmonsen!' she scolded, even as he slid his hands boldly up the sides of her ribcage. 'I want the full works...eggs, bacon, sausages and tomatoes and...and...' Her voice died as Mac bent his head to claim her breast. Hot, languid need coiled from her nipple to her womb, stealing her thoughts away like the most light-fingered pickpocket.

Tunnelling her fingers through his hair, she let herself sink into the pillows behind her. 'Oh, God, Mac...no wonder they call you "the Magician".'

The telephone rang suddenly, the sound stilling them both as its unwanted purring reverberated down the hall.

'Don't answer it.' Green eyes dived pleadingly into blue.

With a slight shake of his head, Mac smiled. 'I have no intention of answering it,' he assured her lazily. 'It's probably a wrong number anyway.' His mouth descended on hers in a swift, demanding kiss. As her bones started to melt all over again, Tara twisted her mouth away.

'What if it's not a wrong number?' The ringing persisted, suddenly seeming even louder. 'What if Mitch is ringing you about work?'

'Then Mitch can go fly a kite because I'm not answering it.'

'Let me get it.'

'What the—? Tara...what the hell do you think you're doing?'

But she was gone from under him before he had time to think, hauling the sheet with her as she went, giving him a tantalising glimpse of a perfectly pert and rounded derrière as she ran out the door.

Just a couple of minutes later she returned, a frown between her pale brows, expression concerned.

Mac's stomach rolled over. 'Who was it? Mitch?' If it was another problem at work, this time his second in command would just have to bite the bullet and deal with it himself. There was no way—none whatsoever—that Mac was breaking up this holiday again. Dammit, he'd sell the business first!

'Not Mitch,' Tara mumbled, touching her hand distractedly to her lips. 'Aunt Beth. She's had an accident and I've got to go home.'

CHAPTER TEN

'WHAT do you mean, it would be better if I stayed at the hotel?' Hardly believing what he was hearing, Mac followed Tara out of the car, frowning fiercely as she fumbled with keys to open the shop door. Her hand shook a little, and she wouldn't look at him.

'Aunt Beth needs me right now and I don't think it's right for you to just move in as soon as her back is turned.' The lock gave, she pushed open the door and stepped into the dim interior filled almost to bursting point with venerable antiques and various *objets d'art*. Mac was close on her heels.

'Do you mind running that by me again?'

Turning wearily, Tara tried to shake off the tiredness that had crept up on her after several hours' travelling and told herself it couldn't hurt to engender a little sane distance between herself and Mac—for a few more days at least. In Ireland it was easier to convince herself that he would keep his promise of not being so work-obsessed—back on their home-ground Tara still wasn't so sure. Beth's accident would take precedence and perhaps give her a little more time to play with until she felt more certain.

'I said—'

'I *know* what you said.' Anger rippled off him and engulfed her. 'I just wanted to make sure I heard you right. Did I just imagine the last few days, Tara, or was it some kind of a dream? After all the things we said, now you try and throw me off like some pesky schoolboy as if our time together meant nothing! I thought we'd agreed that our relationship was firmly back on a permanent basis? How do you square that with banishing me to some quaint little hotel while you live here alone?'

'Just until I sort Aunt Beth out.' Huffing a sigh, she threw her keys onto her aunt's desk and automatically unbuttoned her coat. 'There's going to be a lot to do around here. She has to be the priority.'

'No!' Furious didn't even come close to what he was feeling, Mac realised. Before they'd returned to the UK, they'd talked, made love and talked again…long into the night and through it. They'd both agreed they wanted to be together for good. Now, as far as Mac was concerned, Tara was reneging on their agreement—again keeping him dangling while another convenient excuse presented itself for her to maintain her distance. He'd sacrificed a whole month away from his business to woo her again, to convince her they were meant to be together. He wasn't slinking away now with his tail between his legs until she came to her senses.

'I've been patient with you, Tara. It was never my intention to push you into making a decision either way, but I've given up a lot to be here with you. I just want you to know that I've done that because more than anything I want us to make our marriage work again. You want commitment—you've got commitment! The least we can do now is live together. I don't care whether it's here or at the hotel but to make this work we need to be acting as one.'

Feeling for the desk behind her, Tara lowered herself back onto it, her stomach taking a slow dive to her shoes.

'You've "given up a lot" to be here with me?' Slowly she shook her head. 'You mean your work, don't you?'

As he realised his error and mentally kicked himself for it, Mac's gaze swept the room to buy some time before returning straight to Tara. 'I didn't mean that. It was just a figure of speech.'

'You might fool yourself, Mac, but you don't fool me! You're just itching to get back to your agency, aren't you? You've probably thought of nothing else the whole time you've been here!'

'That's not true!'

'Isn't it?' She walked right up to him and poked him in the chest. Her eyes were spitting icy shards of green and Mac suddenly felt as if his whole world had come crashing down around his ears. *Dammit...*she was right. It wasn't true work had occupied most of his thoughts, because when he was with Tara he thought of nothing else but her, but any moments he found himself at a loose end work undoubtedly crept into his subconscious. He hadn't totally been able to leave it alone, and she was right about that. She was right and he was the biggest bloody fool that had ever lived.

'Don't look at me as if you're about to burst into tears!' Beth scolded her niece. '*I'm* the one who should be crying. I was just about to sell that damn chaise longue at long last and what do I do? Trip up over a chair and fracture my damn knee!' Clearly furious, she helped herself to one of the plump black grapes Tara had arranged in the pretty glass bowl on the hospital locker then chewed it with no apparent enjoyment whatsoever.

'Oh, Aunt.' Sighing, Tara took the older woman's hand in her own, patting it gently on top of the bed as she would a small child's. Although her vitality wasn't dimmed, the accident had visibly taken its toll on her usually exuberant aunt. There were soft grey smudges beneath her eyes, and her face—for once devoid of make-up—was the colour of the palest ivory. Even the eye-catching cerise bed-jacket she wore failed to bring a warmer hue to her complexion. A tug of love welling inside her, Tara's fingers curled more possessively round Beth's hand as if willing her better.

'Please don't worry. Everything's going to be fine. I'm going to look after the shop and all I want you to do is give yourself plenty of time to rest and heal. You'll be out of here in a few days but there's going to be no rushing about like you're used to. You're going to be in a wheelchair for a little while then on crutches, so there'll be nothing for it but to get used to the inactivity. The sooner you comply the sooner you'll be up and about again, like your old self.'

'Since when did the pretty little niece who used to try on my make-up and dress up in my clothes get to be such a wise old woman?' Sniffling, Beth yanked a small lace hankie from beneath her sleeve and pressed it carefully to her nose. Green eyes betrayingly bright, Tara gave the hand she held a brief affectionate squeeze.

'Oh, probably since I made a complete hash of my marriage and ran away to lick my wounds instead of staying and trying to work out what I could do to get my husband back.'

'And where *is* your husband right now? I take it he is still your husband? You didn't succumb to a quickie divorce while you were away?'

Two bright spots of pink shaded Tara's cheekbones. 'Mac and I are still married, and before you ask, I don't know if it's permanent—we still have a few things to work out. Right now I'm just taking one day at a time. As to your first question, Mac is back at the shop, keeping an eye on things. Knowing what a charmer he can be when he tries, he'll probably have most of the contents sold before I get back…including your *damn* chaise longue.'

That brought a smile to Beth's melancholy face. 'Well, if that's the case I'll have to sort out a percentage for him. Seriously, though, won't he have to go back to London at some point?'

And what are you going to do then? Tara heard the unspoken question and shrugged. 'He's got a couple of weeks yet before he goes back. Plenty of time to help me run the shop and do all we can to make things nice and comfy for you when you get out of here.'

'Darling girl, but to be honest I'm more concerned about your welfare than mine. I suppose I have to trust that you know what you're doing as far as that charming husband of yours is concerned. Plainly there's nothing I can do to help right now anyway. And by the way, I do appreciate you cutting short your holiday to come back at such short notice. Perhaps Mac's friend will let you have the house again some time soon?'

As she thought of the long, lazy days they had spent together making love and walking on that gorgeous, deserted beach with white crystal waves lapping on the shore, Tara's inadvertent sigh was laced with hope and longing. But the memory of their row when they'd returned home still featured large in her mind, marring any chance of happiness. 'Who knows?' Smiling briefly, she reached across to the attractive glass bowl to help herself to a handful of grapes.

*   *   *

Skimming through the small, neat pages in her diary, Tara stared at the circled letter 'P' that had been surpassed by five whole days and all the strength seemed to drain from her limbs. Suppressing the urge to scream, cry or tear out her hair, instead she dropped, stunned, onto the toilet seat with its fluffy pink cover and laid her hands wonderingly across her stomach. She hadn't got it wrong as she'd imagined she had. There could be no mistake—even in her heightened state of emotion. Her period was a week overdue and, if that wasn't evidence enough that she was more than likely pregnant, then the slightly spacey feeling she had in her head and her stomach merely confirmed it.

'Great,' she muttered vehemently beneath her breath, 'your timing is perfect, Tara. Just bloody well perfect…' But her words belied her secret joy because inside everything was jumping around as if it were Christmas. To think that Mac and she were going to have another chance to be parents—well, it was an impossible dream come true. *Wasn't it?*

Placing her hand on her right temple, she massaged the pain that had started to throb there. To give him his due, Mac hadn't raised the subject of their reconciliation again. Not since they'd rowed and he'd reluctantly booked himself back into the town's best hotel. It was as though he was biding his time, intuitively waiting for Tara's warring emotions to reach some kind of resolution within herself. But since they'd been back he'd taken charge of practically everything to do with the shop. He'd checked Beth's diary, got in touch with customers and tradespeople to let them know what had happened, rescheduled delivery dates, took care of sales in the shop and even attended a trade fair that Beth had pencilled in on her behalf. Of her own volition Tara had relegated herself to the background, cleaning the flat, doing the laundry, ironing and shopping and generally preparing things for Beth's return. She didn't want her aunt to have any worries to return to, so she'd been glad of the extra help Mac had provided—and it had helped keep their own problems at bay. They'd been skirting politely round each other for days now like skaters dancing around a crack in the ice—both of them reticent for their own reasons to broach the subject of a more permanent arrangement. The fact that Tara was now more than likely pregnant would change all that. Now they would have to talk, and talk seriously.

Returning downstairs to the shop, she was stunned to find the room almost full of customers—*female* customers. His back to her, Mac was seated on the edge of Beth's desk, holding court. Dressed in a navy polonecked sweater and tailored black trousers, the man was a gourmet meal on legs. The four women gathered round him gazed at him as if they'd just been served up the feast of their dreams. Immediately Tara felt irritable.

One of the women, a slim, attractive, fortyish brunette in country tweeds and flats, laughed girlishly at something Mac had said and touched his knee. Tara recognised her as the wife of their local GP—a woman not widely known for her spontaneous sense of humour. A stab of something she hesitated to identify as jealousy shot through her chest, making her ears burn and her heart thump.

'Mac? Can I have a word?'

As she was about a hundred miles up the road past irritable, her words sounded more like a command than a request. Disconcertingly he swivelled towards her and smiled. She felt the impact of it like a grenade landing at her feet.

'What is it, sweetheart?'

Sweetheart? Tara sensed the tenuous threads of her good humour snap like dry spaghetti strands. It didn't help that his new fan club were all gawking at him like adoring teenagers at a boy-band concert.

'I'd like a word *in private*, if you don't mind.' Swinging out the door, she stepped into the small, dimly lit hallway that led to the store room at the back of the shop as well as the stairs to Beth's flat, and waited.

'What's up?' An amused glint in his devastating blue eyes, he dropped his hands to his hips and grinned.

'What the hell do you think you're doing?'

'Out there?' He thumbed behind his back, frowning. 'Isn't it obvious? I'm dealing with the customers.'

'And ''dealing with the customers'' is a euphemism for what? Entertaining sex-starved women who ought to know better?'

He shook his head in disbelief. 'I'm not even going to dignify that with a reply. What's the matter, Tara? Getting a little lonely in that single bed of yours upstairs? I told you I've got a double room back at my hotel.'

Mac knew he'd gone straight for the jugular but he couldn't help it. For six whole days now since their return from Ireland she'd been keeping him at a deliberate distance, as if all the loving that had gone on between them when they were away had been some kind of weakness on her part that she now regretted. Inside he was furious but so far he'd reined in his temper out of respect for Beth. He knew Tara was worried about her aunt, knew too that she was afraid—no, *ter-*

rified—to commit to him again in case they had a repeat of what had happened before, so wisely he'd decided not to push her, to give her more time. But as far as patience was concerned his was suddenly in short supply. What the hell was it going to take to convince her he meant every word he'd said about being totally dedicated to making their relationship a success? He knew he'd almost ruined things by inadvertently indicating that work was still a big priority in his life but he'd already promised to look for a house near by, as well as drastically cutting down his working hours so they could spend more time together. What more did the woman want?

'Don't flatter yourself!' Fists inadvertently clenched by her sides, Tara glared at him with enraged green eyes. 'If I'm lonely, you're not the only fish in the sea, Mac Simmonsen!'

'Insinuating what? That there's someone else on the scene?' Jealousy knifing through him, Mac grabbed her upper arm and held her fast when she would have turned away.

'Of course not!' Biting her lip, Tara cursed her own foolish temper. Trying to make Mac jealous was not the best idea and relations between them—for the last few days anyway—were strained enough. All of a sudden she felt frightened and vulnerable, like a small animal that had gone to ground after a trauma. She was going to have to share her news with him soon because the implications of it were too great for her to bear alone, but first she needed a little more time to shore up her defences. 'I'm feeling a little tired, that's all. I don't want an argument even though you think I'm spoiling for one. I think I'll go and lie down. Do you mind taking care of things in the shop until closing time?'

Releasing her arm, Mac glanced down at his watch. 'No problem. But when closing time comes, I'm coming upstairs to see you. There are a few things we need to get clear on and I'm not leaving until they're dealt with to my complete satisfaction. Is that understood?'

Biting back a resentful retort, Tara corralled her irritation and nodded. 'You can stay for dinner if you like.' As concessions went it was pretty poorly offered and a sense of shame swept over her at her churlishness. 'It's just pasta with a homemade sauce. Nothing fancy.'

Rubbing his hand round his jaw, Mac released a long, slow breath. A *resigned* breath that told Tara his patience was wearing extremely thin and not to push him too far or no more Mr Nice Guy. All of a sudden she longed for those few happy days in Ireland when the only decision they'd had to make was whether or not to get out of bed. Since their coming home, life had quickly got far too serious again.

'Go and lie down.' He briefly touched her hair, the whisper of a smile about his lips. 'I agree you do look tired. Why not let me cook dinner?'

'OK.' At that moment she had neither the will nor the strength to disagree.

'You've hardly eaten a thing.'

'Who are you? My mother?' Pushing away from the dining table, Tara threw down her linen napkin then fled into the living room. Mac found her staring out the window, the room softly illuminated by a small antique lamp in the corner. Not for the first time that evening, he longed to have some insight into what was going on in her head. She'd been as jumpy and as restless as a cat all through dinner, her lovely eyes shying away from direct confrontation whenever he addressed her. He could only pray that her touchiness wasn't because she was trying to find a way to tell him that she couldn't bring herself to reconcile. He had no idea what he'd do if she hit him with that—not when his hopes had been allowed to get so high. Right now he just didn't want to even go there.

'Can I get you anything? Glass of wine? Some brandy perhaps?'

She spun round to regard him, arms crossed protectively in front of her chest in the pale blue denim dress she wore. 'No, thank you.'

Mac scowled. He might have been a waiter asking if her meal had been to her satisfaction for all the interest in her voice.

'OK. Something's going on with you, Tara, and unless you tell me what it is I'm going to get the mother of all headaches trying to fathom it out. What is it? And don't tell me now isn't the right time to ask because I'm not leaving here until I get some answers.' As if to qualify his statement, he dropped down onto the sofa and planted himself there.

If now wasn't the right time to reveal her condition then Tara didn't know when the time would be more right. In a couple of days' time Beth would be home and Tara would need to devote most of her time to looking after her welfare as well as running the shop. She couldn't assume for even a second that Mac would want to continue taking care of that task indefinitely. She was only surprised that he had stuck it out this long. Every day that passed she lived in fear of him telling her he had to go back to work, and once back in London—once back in the hub of his busy, successful agency—who knew when he would make time to see her again?

Her heart feeling as though it were wearing a leaden overcoat, she swallowed down the emotion blocking her throat to release a quivery little sigh.

'Well…I'm not a hundred per cent sure—I mean, I haven't done a proper test yet, but I think I might be…pregnant.'

There, she'd said it and the world hadn't come to an end. Not yet at any rate. Even if Mac had gone awfully quiet and looked as though someone had put him in a trance.

Then he smiled and that drop-dead gorgeous, bring-a-woman-to-her-knees smile just kept on getting wider and wider until Tara almost forgot to breathe.

'I don't know what to say.' After the delivery of that stunning smile of his, his words hit Tara like a smack in the face. That wasn't what she wanted to hear. In her experience, 'don't know' meant doubt, and doubt wasn't reassuring, and dammit! She needed to be reassured everything was going to be all right. Wasn't that what every new mother-to-be longed to know? Especially considering her circumstances, with her previous pregnancy ending in such tragedy.

Engrossed in swirling grey thoughts that were like one of those pea-souper fogs London had been famous for in bygone days, Tara barely registered the fact that Mac had got to his feet and was currently standing in front of her, easing her folded arms down slowly by her sides.

The sensual drift of his cologne registered low in her belly. Desire kindled like a dying camp-fire being stoked back to life. All her senses shifted startlingly into super-alertness. Her eyes stinging, she stared into his beautiful face, anxiety almost choking her. 'We should have used something. It's my fault. I should have insisted you—we—' She didn't finish what she was saying because all of a sudden she found herself pressed hard into Mac's chest and the sensation of that warm, supple strength of his eased into her bones like some soporific herb—stealing away her pain, enveloping her in almost unspeakable tenderness.

'I didn't know what to say because I was overwhelmed,' Mac was crooning against her ear, his warm breath instigating delightful little shock waves all along her lobe. 'It's wonderful news, Tara. I feel like a kid who's just got everything he wanted for Christmas!'

Her arms slipped round his waist and held on tight. Raising her head, she gazed questioningly up at him.

'Then you don't mind?'

'Mind? Woman, are you completely mad?' Laughing, he lifted her off her feet and swung her round.

'Stop, Mac! You're making me dizzy.' Her heart racing with myriad different emotions, Tara clung to him a little to get her bearings before gently breaking away. 'In light of what's happened, I'm not going to pretend that I can manage on my own. Although Gabriel didn't live, I was perfectly aware all through my pregnancy that a child needs two parents. It wasn't easy being on my own and faced with the reality of being a single mother. This time I want to do things right but I can only do that if I'm sure you're going to stay the course. I know we can only take one day at a time... I'm not looking for cast-iron guarantees. But I need to know you really mean it when you say that the baby and I are what you want. I don't want your work to take over when you go back and for you to gradually forget the promises you made.'

Contemplating her sad, lovely face, Mac mused again how he could have walked out on her that first time. It scared him to remember how he'd allowed his work to get such a hold on his life. Since taking this extended leave, he'd slowly begun to realise the alternatives to living such a crazy, frenetic existence—even if he'd still been resisting them. Life in the fast lane might sound glamorous to some but Mac knew it was hell on your emotions and your health, so no more. When he went back he was going to start handing over the reins to Mitch. He didn't just want to be there for Tara when she had the baby, he wanted to be there for most of her pregnancy—to watch over her and look out for her and make sure she got the best possible care that his hard-earned money could buy.

'I swear I'm going to keep every promise I ever make to you from now on,' he told her, his voice husky. 'I might not have been the best husband in the past but you won't be able to fault me in the future. Well…not most of the time anyway.' Grinning sheepishly, he coaxed her stiff body into his arms. 'We're going to be the best parents. Our baby's not going to want for anything.'

And what about me, Mac? Tara longed to ask him. *Your love is all I want. Am I going to go on wanting for that? What my baby and I need the most is love and it's the one thing that all the money in the world can't buy.*

'Anyway.' Wriggling out of his arms, willing the tears not to flow, she forced a wobbly little smile. 'I want to ring the hospital, see how Beth's doing. Thanks for cooking dinner…even if I didn't eat it.'

His frown made the slight ridges in his forehead more evident. 'And that's something that's also going to change around here…your eating habits. They're atrocious. You don't eat enough to keep a bird alive. Tomorrow morning I'm going to find a good nutritionist as well as a good obstetrician and book you in for some appointments.' Grabbing his jacket off the arm of a chair where he'd left it, Mac shrugged it on, raked his fingers through his hair and smiled. 'I'll be here first thing to open the shop but we'll close for the afternoon. There's a lot to do—including a visit to the estate agents to look for a house. Goodnight, Tara. Sleep well. You know where I am if you need me.'

Feeling dazed, she was still looking at the door he'd closed behind him long after he'd left.

Her feet hurt. Lord knew she should have resisted wearing strappy little sandals with killer heels but nothing else went with the beautiful pink and silver knit dress that Mac had surprised her with and asked her to wear to dinner. Now she surreptitiously slipped them off under the table and prayed she'd be able to put them on again when it was time to leave. He'd brought her to London, to one of the most expensive and stylish restaurants in the capital, where the *maître d'* had addressed him like a long-lost friend. 'To celebrate,' he'd told Tara—adding that it had been a long time since he'd felt like celebrating anything.

During the afternoon beforehand they'd visited an 'exclusive homes' estate agent and now Mac had a file of beautiful homes in the county to visit just as soon as they had picked out the ones that sounded suitable and could arrange viewing. In Tara's diary she had two new appointments, one with a recommended nutritionist locally and the other with a top obstetrician in Harley Street. Every time she glanced at the latter her tummy would flip into a perfect somersault and the whole day she'd felt as if she'd wandered into someone else's dream. Now she sat opposite Mac at a perfect oval table with beautiful place settings and silver candelabra, in a secluded alcove away from the main hub of the restaurant—attentive waiters at their beck and a bottle of crystal champagne on ice. If she weren't so averse to pain she'd pinch herself.

'I don't think I've ever seen you look more beautiful.' Raising his glass thoughtfully to his lips, Mac took a sip of wine then placed the glass carefully back down on the table.

'It's the dress.' Feeling herself blush, Tara fingered the plunging neckline, wishing fervently that it didn't plunge quite so low. Her breasts weren't large by any means but she still felt like Nell Gwyn with so much creamy flesh on show—flesh that she would rather have kept hidden. It was obvious that Mac didn't share her opinion because his highly appreciative blue eyes kept dipping to her cleavage as though the Koh-i-noor diamond resided there. She didn't dare imagine what he was thinking. The fact that he looked pretty gorgeous himself didn't help. In his impeccable dark grey suit, maroon shirt and black tie, his golden hair swept back almost rakishly from his handsome face, he was one potent, sexy male and Tara warned herself to go easy on the alcohol because her senses were already close to sensation meltdown.

'No.' A flicker of a knowing smile briefly raised the corners of his mouth. 'It's the *woman* in the dress. No question.'

'You don't scrub up too badly yourself.'

He laughed out loud, the inadvertently sensual timbre intruding disconcertingly on her ability to think, to string one or two words together coherently. Anybody would think she was a lovesick teenager out on her first proper date.

'I've been thinking of renting a house near your aunt's—just until we can buy a place of our own. As comfortable as my hotel undoubtedly is, I don't want to stay there indefinitely. More to the point, I don't want us to be apart any more. It's time we were together again...permanently.'

She knew he was right but it didn't stop her heart from almost thudding right out of her chest. She loved him so much that she just couldn't bear it if, when they finally moved in together, things didn't work out. To soothe her scattered nerves, she took a deep gulp of dry, crisp champagne.

'Easy on the alcohol, baby.' There was a brooding intensity to his gaze that made Tara curl her toes in her stockinged feet. When he looked at her like that she forgot those last few doubts and felt that he truly did love her. That he didn't just want her because he was trying to right past wrongs, or because she was once again having his baby. Gazing unseeingly past his impressively broad shoulders, she twirled the fragile stem of her wine glass between her fingers.

'I know what I'm doing.'

'I want you to stay healthy during this pregnancy. I know we're having wine and champagne, but after tonight I don't want you to have any more alcohol.'

She stiffened her spine, her green eyes flashing. 'I'm quite capable of judging when I can or can't dr—'

'Mac, darling! I thought it was you! Patrice and I— Remember my sister, Patrice? We were just talking about you. We were wondering if you had managed to persuade that stubborn little wife of yours to give you a divorce so that you could finally be free. Oh, I'm sorry, I didn't see your lovely companion there—aren't you going to introduce us, Mac?'

CHAPTER ELEVEN

THE French girl was a dead ringer for a young Audrey Hepburn. Exquisitely attired in an aubergine-coloured little satin dress that skimmed her virtually non-existent hips, and smelling of some almost overpoweringly gorgeous fragrance, she made Tara feel like some ill-coordinated blowsy blonde in comparison. But more than that her senses were reeling with the impact of the woman's deliberately insulting phraseology. 'Stubborn little wife'? Was that how Mac had referred to her?

Her startled gaze froze into his. She heard the bated breath he suddenly released and knew he was discomfited by the appearance of his ex-girlfriend, because as sure as hens hatched baby chicks this had to be the famous Amelie.

He didn't bother to rise to his feet as politeness dictated. Instead, he coolly looked the French girl over as though it was beneath him even to deign a reply. Tara saw the faint flush of scarlet beneath the other woman's perfect make-up and actually felt sorry for her.

'It would have been nice to be able to say I was glad to see you again, Amelie, but under the circumstances that would be stretching the bounds of credibility too far. Why don't you just go on back and find your sister and allow Tara and myself to enjoy our dinner in peace?'

'So I was right? This is your wife. Have you managed to get her pregnant yet, Mac? You were in such a hurry to embrace fatherhood. She certainly has a healthy ''bloom'' about her that makes one think of a mother-to-be.' Dark, flashing eyes skimmed scathingly down to Tara's cleavage and back up to her face. 'All that creamy white flesh. Makes one think of a serving wench. I am not sure I would want to sacrifice my figure to be in the same position.'

'Call that a figure?' Throwing her napkin down on the table, Tara got to her feet. 'I've seen telegraph poles with more curves! If you'll excuse me, I suddenly feel the urge for a change of air. Nice of you to drop by and chat to my husband and me…sorry, what *was* your name?' And with a dismissive toss of her head and a sexy little shimmy as she passed, Tara wound her way past tables and waiters in her stockinged feet to find the ladies' room, and practically every male head in the restaurant turned her way to mark her progress.

Mac didn't even bother to try and disguise his amusement. Furious, Amelie murmured an insult in the expressive language of her homeland then stalked away as regally as her anger allowed her. Once he was alone again, Mac leaned back in his seat, loosened his tie, then let out a long, slow breath. If he could have spared Tara Amelie's insult he would have—but then his pretty blonde wife had more than bested his ex. He was both surprised and turned on by her unexpected display of chutzpah. The girl he had married had blossomed from the shy twenty-two-year-old he'd first met into an assertive, confident young woman who didn't just turn heads because of her looks—but also because there was an almost commandingly forthright air about her that made people pay attention. He remembered that she'd told him how she'd lost confidence after the loss of their baby, and felt a deep surge of gratitude that she'd obviously started to regain it. Curling his fingers round the stem of his wine glass, Mac knew that he was head over heels in love with her. A future without Tara in it just wasn't a future worth contemplating as far as he was concerned. And now they were going to become parents. Silently blessing the fates for giving him this second chance at happiness, he made a vow that whatever happened he wasn't going to screw it up.

Ten minutes later, he considered his watch with concern. Catching the eye of a passing waiter, he asked if someone could go and check on his wife in the ladies' room because she hadn't returned to their table. In an effort to stem the anxiety clenching his gut, Mac took another sip of wine and told himself to relax.

In the scented powder room with its gleaming basins and shiny mirrors, Tara yanked several more tissues out of the floral box like a conjuror pulling handkerchiefs out of his sleeve, and handed them to the pretty brunette sobbing in the wicker chair in front of her. Sniffling, the young woman gratefully took hold of the wodge of tissue then noisily blew her nose. 'I said some awful things,' she murmured, big brown eyes shimmering up at Tara. 'I said if he loved work so much, why didn't he just move in there? I'd be better off with a flatmate—at least I'd have someone to go out with now and then. He just glared at me and said I should be more understanding, that he was working so hard for me—for us—to give our baby a better future. Then he w-walked out of the restaurant and l-left me here.'

'You're pregnant?'

The young woman nodded miserably. 'I was so happy when I found out but now I just w-want to d-die.' Collapsing into another bout of uncontrollable sobbing, she covered her face with her hands, her mascara caking her eyelashes in a way that made her look like a sad little circus clown.

Dropping down onto her haunches in front of her, Tara smoothed back the girl's softly disarrayed brown hair then gently prised her hands away from her face. 'What's your name?' she asked.

'Sinead.'

'Well, Sinead, I'm Tara and I'm pregnant too. If it's any consolation I know what you're going through. I also had a lot of disagreements with my husband about his dedication to his work and instead of being open to compromise I moped around feeling hard-done-by and sorry for myself. In some ways I was right to get on his case but in others I wasn't. The point is…' She paused to realise just how far she'd come down the road from misery to happiness and could have hugged herself with the delight of it—despite the French girl's bitchy insinuations that Mac only wanted Tara because he wanted to become a father. That wasn't even close to the truth. The truth was that whenever Mac looked her way these days the love he felt for her was shiningly obvious, even if he hadn't actually said the words yet. 'The point is that you have to keep talking. Keep the lines of communication open. Don't let resentment and anger make you do something you might live to regret. Your baby needs two parents—two parents who love each other and will give him the best home he could wish for. Trust me—if you both calm down a little and celebrate the things that attracted you to each other in the first place, you'll be just fine. I promise.'

Sinead had stopped crying. Patting the crumpled tissue beneath her eyes, she managed a tremulous smile.

'Paul—that's my husband—he's got a great sense of humour, you know? Always making me laugh. We're really good together when we're not arguing.' She gave a sad little shrug and for a moment looked lost in thought. 'We came out tonight to celebrate the news of my pregnancy. He brought his mobile phone with him and when it went off a few minutes ago—it was someone from work wanting him to come in early tomorrow. Well, I'm afraid I just flipped. That's when I said he should move his things into work so he wouldn't have to come home at all. He's never walked out on me before. He was so angry...what if he never comes back?'

Seeing the tears welling again in those huge brown eyes, Tara squeezed Sinead's hand and smiled. 'Of course he'll come back,' she said confidently—secretly praying she was right. 'He'll walk up and down a bit and get his knickers in a twist but then he'll cool down again and come back. Do you really think he'd want to miss a slap-up meal in celebration of your baby?'

Sinead shook her head, sighing heavily.

'Look, why don't you come back with me to my table? You can sit with me and Mac and chat to us until Paul comes back. How about it?'

'Mac's your husband?'

'Stands for Macsen. His father was Norwegian.'

'Are you sure he w-won't mind?' Slowly Sinead stood up, glancing in the mirror to attend to her disarrayed hair.

'Of course he won't mind.'

Waiting until Sinead had tidied her hair and reapplied her smudged make-up, Tara was about to lead the way out of the ladies' room when a smartly attired waitress popped her head round the door and asked if either of them went by the name of Mrs Simmonsen, because a Mr Simmonsen was getting rather anxious about her welfare and their meal was about to be served.

'Nice young couple.' As he glanced at Tara snuggled up in the passenger seat beside him, Mac's gaze slipped appreciatively down to the shapely thigh lovingly outlined by the pink and silver knit dress and couldn't prevent the low throb of heat in his groin. His fingers automatically tightened round the steering wheel as he forced himself to concentrate on the dark strip of road ahead.

'Lovely,' Tara murmured, turning to regard him. 'I was so glad Paul didn't leave her stranded. Sinead was breaking her heart over him in the ladies'.'

Mac said nothing for several long seconds. Shifting in her seat, Tara prompted hesitantly, 'Mac? Is everything all right?'

'Shades of you and me five years ago, huh? Funny how listening to what Paul had to say about his work made me realise what a fool I was then.'

'It was good of you to talk to him the way you did. I think it really helped him to see things in a different light, to make priorities—remind him that his wife needed some of his time too. I really think those two will work it out, don't you?'

'Hope so. I was worried about you, you know? When you were taking so long to come out of the ladies', I mean. I thought something might be wrong.'

Registering the sudden tension in the line of his strong shoulders, Tara scooted up into a proper sitting position. Her heart gave a little jolt when she realised what he was referring to.

'You mean with the baby?' She hurried to reassure him. 'Everything's fine. I'm feeling good. I did one of those proper tests this morning—I got a kit from the chemist's just to confirm things and I'm definitely pregnant and I'm definitely OK. Any day now the morning sickness should kick in but, having been through it once before, I know what to expect, so I'm not too worried.'

For answer, Mac reached out and laid his hand on her knee. 'I don't want you to worry about anything. You're seeing Dr Chamberlain on Monday morning and he'll give you a complete check-up. If you have any particular concerns you can discuss it with him.'

'Mac?'

'What is it?' He withdrew his hand to concentrate on manoeuvring the car round a sudden sharp bend in the road.

'Just because—because Gabriel died the way he did, it doesn't mean the same thing's going to happen to this baby...you know that, don't you? The obstetrician at the hospital told me the odds of it happening twice were practically nil.'

Anxiety and regret clutched at Mac's chest, making it almost difficult to breathe. 'That's good to know. Still, I'm going to make sure that you have the best care possible—we won't be taking any chances—and there'll definitely be no shifting heavy stuff around in the antique shop. If Beth needs help, she can ask me. By the way, tomorrow I've got a possible house for rent to go and view. I thought you might like to come.'

'You haven't forgotten Beth's coming home in the afternoon?'

'Seeing as I'm going to pick her up, why would I forget?'

'Just checking.'

'Tara?'

'Hmm?' Snuggling back down in the luxurious leather seat, she glanced at him with a sleepy gaze.

'I'm sorry about Amelie showing up at the restaurant like that. I'm even sorrier for the things she said. You know she only said them because she was mad at me?'

'I worked that out for myself, Mac. Anyway...I could handle it.'

'Damn right.' Mac was still smiling as he pointed the car towards home.

Mac strolled into the living room of their new rented house to find his wife reaching up to the topmost shelf of a bookcase, diligently polishing it with a duster, her hips wiggling delightfully. She was wearing a short, tight black skirt, a hot-pink blouse, black hosiery and pumps, and as soon as he set eyes on the tempting little package she made Mac's famed ability to think on his feet vanish in less than a second. Catching the citrus and musk tones of her fragrance, he paused to take a steadying breath before walking up behind her and sliding his arms possessively round her waist.

'You smell gorgeous, you know that?' Nuzzling her neck, he felt himself hardening the instant she leant back against him, pressing her bottom provocatively into his groin.

'Hmm...so do you.' With a breathless little sigh, Tara pivoted in his arms, her clear green eyes gazing hungrily up at the sensually lazy smile hijacking his delectable lips. Unable to resist such temptation, she stood on tiptoe to deliver several small, well-aimed kisses, her teeth tugging playfully on his lower lip, encouraging him to open for her so she could delve into his heat. Put it down to hormones or just healthy old lust—Tara didn't care which—all she knew was that since she had moved back in with Mac she couldn't leave the man alone. Not that he seemed to be complaining.

'Take off your clothes.' With a predatory little growl she settled her small hands on his lapels, starting to ease his jacket down over his shoulders, surprised and disappointed when his hand suddenly clamped her wrist to stop her.

'Hey…I thought it was *my* antecedents who were famed for pillaging and ravishing?' he teased, blue eyes dancing. The picture his words conjured up in her mind had Tara's nipples aching and her blood temperature soaring off the scale.

'Well, then…' Sliding her free hand into his hair, she deliberately lowered her voice to a seductive purr. 'Why don't you put your money where your mouth is and show me how it's done?'

He groaned, kissed her hard then abruptly released her. 'This won't do, Tara.'

'Mac? What's wrong?' Had she overstepped the mark? What wouldn't do? she fretted. Did sexually assertive females turn him off? Since they'd got back together she'd been slowly but surely letting her guard down, revealing sides to her personality previously kept under wraps, telling herself to trust him, believe in him. He was a good man. Mac wouldn't hurt her the way he had before—he cared about her too much for that ever to happen again. But, that aside, she felt herself retreating behind a sudden wave of doubt, terrified she'd done or said something wrong to make him withdraw. Crossing her arms protectively across her chest, she waited anxiously for him to explain.

She heard him swear softly beneath his breath. At least she thought he was swearing—it was difficult to tell when the language he'd used was Norwegian. 'I think we need to lay down some ground rules,' he said, scratching his head, as if desperately searching for a solution to whatever was bothering him.

'Ground rules?' Even more puzzled, Tara uncrossed her arms and dropped her hands to her hips instead.

'I don't think it's good for you to get too over-stimulated,' he replied, expression torn. 'Too much sexual activity probably isn't good for the baby.'

Tara would have laughed out loud if he didn't look so damned in earnest. 'And where did you hear that?' she asked, striving to keep her voice light—not an easy feat when rising hysteria was threatening.

'It makes sense, doesn't it?' Doubt flitted across his handsome features and something warm and precious sneaked into Tara's heart and made a home there.

'Does it?' A bubble of mirth had her biting her lip to keep from smiling.

'Anyway, Dr Chamberlain said it was important that you get plenty of rest for the first three months. I don't want you tiring yourself out with household chores or things like that. I've already been on to a domestic agency to hire someone to come in once a day and do a little light cleaning and some ironing. Now, why don't you just put your feet up and I'll make you one of those nice fruit teas we bought at the health shop?'

'Dammit, Mac, don't patronise me! I don't want fruit tea! I absolutely loathe the stuff. Give me a proper brew any day in preference to that scented water! And anyway, tea's not the issue here, is it?' Warming to her subject, Tara strode up and down as if the activity somehow helped to release all the frustrating thoughts that were backing up in her brain.

'You've been treating me like spun glass ever since I told you I was pregnant. It's lovely of you but really I don't need a fuss. Being pregnant isn't the same as being ill, Mac, and I do know how to take care of myself. We've got a cupboard full of all kinds of weird and wonderful items from the health shop that I wouldn't even eat if I were stranded on a desert island for a year! I'm longing for some proper food…fish and chips, sausages and mash, curry and rice. And if this healthy regime you've put me on isn't bad enough—now you're trying to curtail the one thing that makes me really happy. *That's* what won't do, Mac! Got it?'

God, but she was beautiful when she was angry. Staring at his wife with all the intense concentration of a child gazing through a sweet-shop window, Mac endeavoured to get his rapid breathing under control. No matter how much he desired her, he thought fiercely, no matter how many ice-cold showers he had to endure over the next couple of months—it would be a small price to pay for him to know that Tara was absolutely healthy and out of any potential danger. No matter how persuasive her arguments—and he thrilled to the fact that she seemed to desire him as much as he did her—he wouldn't jeopardise the baby just because he couldn't keep his lust under control. This wasn't a first pregnancy for Tara. Her first one had ended in the worst tragedy a mother could imagine. It was fine that the doctors had reassured her that the likelihood of it happening twice was rare indeed, but even a half-percent chance that it could happen again was greater odds than Mac wanted to contemplate.

'We both have to be sensible, Tara…that's all I'm

saying. Now, if you don't want tea, how about a drive over to Beth's to see how she's doing? I don't like the idea of her being on her own in the shop in a wheel-chair. I know Peter Trent said he'd keep an eye on things but I'm sure she could use some familiar com-pany, aren't you?'

Swallowing down her frustration, Tara swept past her husband to the door. 'I just hate it when you're so damned thoughtful and reasonable!' she uttered and Mac heard her stomp up the stairs as if it was his head she'd like to be stomping on. Shaking his head with amusement, he mused in wonder at the complexities of living with a woman ruled by her hormones and de-cided that—apart from making love—the experience was the most fun he'd had in a very long time.

'He's been such a sweetie, I can't tell you.' Beth sipped her scented cup of Earl Grey tea, her smile guarded as she viewed them both across her desk, her gaze occa-sionally meandering distractedly out the window to the bookshop across the road. A small spurt of amazement made Tara lift her brows and look searchingly at Mac. He merely grinned and shrugged those powerful shoul-ders of his as if to say 'your guess is as good as mine.'

'We *are* talking about Peter Trent here? ''Mr-boring-head - in - a - book - needing - a - personality - transplant - wouldn't - look - twice - if - a - woman - walked - into - his - shop-naked''? *Your* words, not mine, let me hasten to remind you.'

Blushing as delicately as a young girl, Beth placed her cup carefully in its decorative porcelain saucer and noisily cleared her throat. 'Did I say that? Just goes to show, one should never judge a book by its cover—if you'll pardon the pun. Anyway, let's just say we had the opportunity to get to know each other a little better during his visits to the hospital. I don't mind being the first to confess that I grossly misjudged the man. We've got quite a lot in common, if you really want to know...we like the same kind of films, we both love the theatre and of course the ballet—*and* we share a love of Thai cuisine. In fact, tomorrow evening Peter is taking me out to my favourite Thai restaurant in St Edmunds for dinner—so the pair of you can stop worrying unnecessarily about me and get on with your own lives. Peter's just across the road and he checks in regularly to see if I need anything.'

'Are you sure you're ready to go out? You've not long got out of hospital.' Glancing doubtfully at the thick plaster cast peeping out from beneath her aunt's mid-calf-length dress, Tara had her reservations.

'Peter says we shall manage quite nicely. If you can come over about an hour beforehand and help me into my best frock, I'll be absolutely fine.'

'Of course I'll come and help you.'

'Good. That's settled, then.'

'Well, great. That's great, Beth. But if you should need anything in the meantime, anything at all—you know where we are.' If uncertainty crept into her voice, Tara couldn't help it. Things seemed to be changing so fast—things that a mere month ago she could never have dreamed. A girl needed a little time to acclimatise at least.

'I notice you're using the term "we" quite a lot.' Beth's eyes twinkled. 'Do I take it all's well in the Simmonsen household?'

'Apart from Mac fussing over me like a mother hen, you mean?' Endeavouring to sound nonchalant, Tara nevertheless slid her gaze tenderly across to Mac as he stood beside her. As he grinned back at her, she felt that familiar 'where's my parachute?' drop in her stomach when his electric blue eyes collided warmly with hers.

'I'm glad to hear it. That's just what every mother-to-be needs—a good man.' She looked pointedly at Mac and a kind of unspoken agreement flowed between them that Tara wasn't privy to. 'Don't complain, darling. And by the way, I hope you're taking all your vitamins and things and eating sensibly. Is she, Mac?'

'You know that old saying? You can lead a horse to water but you can't make it drink? I think that just about sums up the current situation.' Smoothing back a drifting strand of gold from his forehead, he smiled wryly at both women.

'I know she can be terrifically stubborn when she wants to be,' Beth remarked fondly. 'But now the baby's coming I think she'll agree she needs to be sensible.'

Tara grimaced. 'Sensible? Do you know how much I'm beginning to loathe that word? I'm going to have a baby—not join a nunnery!'

'Amen to that.' Absorbing his wife's indignant glare, Mac was gratified that he had a strong ally in her aunt. Maybe between the two of them they could get Tara to see that they were only acting in her best interests? Stealing a glance at her peeved expression, he could see they were seriously going to have their work cut out.

CHAPTER TWELVE

'STOP scowling at me! You know it will give you major wrinkles when you're older? Come on and dance. I haven't dragged you up to town to spend the night propping up the bar.'

'I should never have listened to you,' Raj replied, his expression strained as he surveyed the packed dance floor in the club. 'Sometimes you persuade me to act against my better judgement and this is definitely one of those times. What's your husband going to think when I drop you home later?'

Squashing down the niggling spurt of anxiety that had been dogging her ever since she'd got the notion to ask Raj to take her dancing, Tara tossed her head dismissively, telling herself that Mac would just have to like it or lump it because she wasn't going to curtail her very normal and natural impulses for anybody. OK, so she'd taken the coward's way out and told him she was popping round a friend's for a girly night in, watching a video or two. But sometimes a woman had to do what a woman had to do, and the mood Mac had been in lately he would only read her the Riot Act—*especially* if he found out she'd gone out with Raj. It didn't matter that their friendship was strictly on the level. Mac simply didn't believe that men and women could just be friends.

'Why don't you just let *me* worry about Mac?' Pulling him to his feet, Tara urged Raj onto the dance floor. As the compulsive bass of one of the latest dance records throbbed loudly around the room, she surrendered to her need to move her body, conveniently banishing anything else to the far regions of her mind.

Raj switched off the car engine then swivelled in his seat to look at Tara. She'd slept pretty much most of the way home, snuggled up in the passenger seat beside him like a child, her soft blonde hair mussed and the skirt of her short black embroidered dress crinkled mid-thigh. Not for the first time Raj noticed that she had very good legs—the kind of legs that could make a man seriously hot under the collar. Without a doubt she'd been the prettiest girl at the club, eliciting a fiercely protective feeling in him whenever he spied an interested male homing in. Sighing deeply, he had to admit he was more than a little jealous of Mac. Perhaps that was why he had gone against his own better judgement and agreed to take her out tonight without her husband's knowledge? His father, Sanjay, would kill him if he ever found out, but not before his mother's fierce tirade burst his eardrums.

'Tara? Tara, wake up! We're home.' He shook her a little desperately, his heart racing when she peeled open those mesmerising, long-lashed green eyes and smiled.

'Hmm.' Stretching and yawning at the same time, she manoeuvred herself upright, peering through the windscreen at the large red-bricked house at the end of the gravel drive, Mac's gleaming sedan parked sedately outside. Anxiety settled like a bowling ball in the pit of her stomach. Now she was for it. Unless, of course, Mac had gone to bed and was hopefully sound asleep. Yeah, and Queen Elizabeth would abdicate tomorrow...

'Thank you, Raj. I had the best time. You are an angel.' Leaning towards him, she gave him a generous peck on the cheek.

Her companion retreated as if he'd been stung. 'Don't do that! Your husband might see.' He craned his neck to see if Mac was looking out of one of several leaded windows. The house was large and impressive—the kind of house that he intended to have one day for himself and his new wife.

'What's to see?' she asked, shrugging. 'He knows we're only friends.'

'Sometimes, Tara, you take too much for granted.' Beneath his smooth dark skin, heat shaded Raj's jaw.

'What? You're saying you're *not* my friend?'

'Don't twist my words!' Clearly frustrated, he slammed the centre of the steering wheel with the flat of his hand. 'What I'm saying is you make too familiar with me sometimes. I'm only a man when all is said and done and you're an extremely attractive woman. Such familiarity can lead to dangerous situations if people aren't careful.'

She knew what he was saying and even felt slightly ashamed that she had put him in a potentially compromising position, but first of all she heard his clear admonishment for restraint and she saw red. It had been over a week now since her husband had made love to her and sexual frustration and pure driving need for more intimate contact was slowly driving her round the bend. Now her best friend and supposed ally was suggesting even more self-control. Tara decided she just couldn't handle any of it.

'You know something, Raj? Sometimes in life you just have to take risks. Would Ellen MacArthur have sailed solo round the globe if she'd been ''careful''?

Would Edmund Hillary have got to the top of Mount Everest? Would I be having another baby with Mac if I didn't risk my heart and my pride? Think about it. Thanks for bringing me home. I'll be seeing you.'

Standing outside the oak front door, Tara waved as Raj pulled away and drove through the black and gold railings back onto the road, her mouth dry and trepidation knotting her spine. It was one thing being bold on a whim—quite another facing the consequences of that boldness. Especially when she now had deep reservations about her actions. Mac was only trying to do what was best for her. He wasn't deliberately trying to make life difficult because he suggested she slow down a little. He was thinking about her and the baby. The least he deserved was the truth about where she'd been. 'So much for bravado.' Muttering disparagingly to herself, she slid her key into the lock and let herself in.

The house was in silence except for the comforting tick of the Victorian mantel clock that Beth had given them as a housewarming present emanating from the front room. Leaving her purse on a handy side-table, Tara kicked off her shoes, deposited her coat on the staircase balustrade then ventured slowly towards the sound.

'So you finally decided to come home?'

His deceptively velvet tones announced Mac's presence as surely as if someone had come up to her and rung a bell in her ear. Heart thudding, Tara threaded her fingers through her already tousled fringe, staring in shocked disbelief at his seated figure in one of the winged armchairs by the fireplace. Back-lit by the glowing embers of the fire, his skin appeared almost golden, his eyes a spellbindingly sapphire blue. He was dressed in faded blue denims and a dove-grey T-shirt that highlighted the steely cords of muscle in his biceps; he looked arrogantly, fiercely male, and Tara couldn't prevent the small shiver of purely female appreciation that slipped like golden syrup down her spine.

'You didn't have to wait up.' Was that her voice? Or had Minnie Mouse taken possession of her vocal cords?

'No?' Rising to his feet, he stood in front of the fire, jeans riding low on his lean, tight hips, expression inexorably austere. 'Tell me...did you have a good time with your...friend?'

Her aching feet could easily attest to that, Tara thought, grimacing. She'd all but danced her legs off. Even Raj had complained she'd hardly sat down all night. But that was what music did for her: it touched her soul, made her want to move to its beat—once a dancer, always a dancer. 'Yeah, I had a good time. But now I'm tired, so if you don't mind I think I'll go to bed.'

'Not so fast.'

As she moved towards the door Mac sprung like a panther, reaching her in an instant, his hand locking onto her arm and spinning her back round. 'Tell me where you really were, Tara, because I know damn well you didn't wear that dress to spend the evening in front of a girlfriend's TV, watching videos.'

If he had seen the dress before she'd left Tara would never have left the house. As it was she'd had the foresight to slip on her long black coat when she'd bid him goodbye for the evening.

Knowing lying wasn't an option and despising herself for even considering it, she pulled angrily at her captive arm, scowling fiercely at Mac when he wouldn't let go. 'I don't know why you're making such a big deal out of this! I was with Raj, OK? My friend. Since I've become pregnant you won't let me do a damn thing and I've had all this pent-up energy I didn't know what to do with so I asked Raj to take me to London to a nightclub. All I wanted to do was listen to some music and dance. Is that such a crime?'

'You lied to me.'

'Not deliberately. I just didn't want you to get upset.'

'And I'm not upset now?' His question was remarkably restrained, considering the muscle that ticked in his jaw. Tara wasn't so foolish as to underestimate him. She knew underneath that deceptively calm façade he was seething…and rightly so.

'I can see you're not happy.' Her arm was tingling where he held it—little sparks of electricity shooting into her bloodstream, making her feel slightly giddy. Blast! What a time to feel aroused.

'Damn right I'm not happy. You're pregnant, Tara. You need to take care of yourself, to rest. Going to a nightclub and dancing the night away flouts everything the doctor said about taking things easier. Just what the devil got into you? And to get another man to take you… What the hell did he think he was playing at?' Her 'friend,' she'd called him, and Mac's heart had gone wild with jealousy. What exactly did that mean? He didn't care if it was true the guy had some arranged marriage in India—if he had testosterone pumping through his veins he had every chance of being attracted to Tara. In that sexy little black dress she was wearing with its generous V-neck front and back, the woman looked like an angelic blonde siren. The man who didn't find her appealing would have to be dead.

'Don't go blaming Raj.'

'You seem pretty eager to jump to his defence. No man in his right mind would even contemplate taking another man's wife out dancing without his knowledge! Does your ''friendship'' extend to sharing his bed? Or maybe you made out in the car? Answer me, Tara! I want to know.'

She went very quiet. Inside her mind was racing. 'I don't believe you just said that. How can you turn something so innocent into something so...so *dirty*? I despise you for that!'

'You don't wriggle out of it so easily,' he replied, voice deadly calm. 'Answer the question.'

The force of her emotions made her tremble. 'No! I do not sleep—and have never slept—with Raj Singh! *I'm* the fool who's been celibate for five years—I know for a fact you can't attest to the same self-restraint! But this isn't about blaming and accusations, is it, Mac? This is about trust—or lack of it. I've trusted you enough to move in with you again, to believe we can have a real marriage. How can we ever expect to achieve that when you clearly don't even trust me to leave the house on my own? And to even entertain such a crass notion as Raj and me sleeping together! Didn't you hear what I said about him being engaged to be married? It all points to the fact that you don't even trust me to take care of myself! You've been treating me like a child since I told you about the baby. Do you really believe I'd do something reckless that might endanger this pregnancy? I know how to take care of things, Mac. What do you think I've been doing for the past five years? Did you think I'd just stop living because you walked out the door? My life may not seem terribly exciting to you but I'm the one who makes the choices in it. I'm a grown woman—not a little girl.'

A muscle pulsed in the side of Mac's temple. Registering her passionate words, he knew he'd made a gross error. She'd never given him the slightest reason to mistrust her. The Tara he knew had always been delightfully open and honest—even if sometimes he didn't like hearing what she had to say because he knew it reflected badly on him. The fact that she'd lied to him tonight about where she was going must mean he'd pushed her into such a corner that she'd had no alternative but to act as she did.

'Raj only took me because I begged him. If dancing makes me happy, how can it hurt anything? It's part of who I am, Mac. Would you want me to change that? I can't just sit at home and play the little woman. I did that to some extent the first time round, sitting at home night after night—giving up my social life in deference to your work. I don't intend to do that a second time. I have to burn off some of this excess energy some way.'

'Then why the hell couldn't you ask me to take you dancing?'

'Would you have?'

'I'd take you anywhere you wanted so long as I knew you were safe.'

'Right.' She bit her lip, her eyes sliding away from the full force of his penetrating gaze. 'Maybe next time I will. But you've got to trust me. You've got to stop being so damn controlling!'

'Controlling, am I?' Mac released her arm, watching her flex it a little to get the blood pumping properly again. Instantly he regretted holding on to her so tightly.

'If the cap fits…'

'So be it.' Blue eyes pinning her to the spot, Mac tilted his jaw towards her.

Why couldn't she have just kept quiet? Tara thought unhappily. But it wasn't right that men thought they had the monopoly on sexual frustration. Her breathing shallow, she raised her gaze defiantly to his. 'What the hell is that supposed to mean?'

'That's for me to know and you to find out.' Giving her no warning, Mac reached for her, lifted her into his arms and carried her towards the stairs. Tara felt his steely strength enfold her and was torn between tearing him off a strip for his high-handedness and simply acquiescing to myriad deliciously seductive sensations that were rippling through her body.

'Put me down!' she ordered, but even to her own ears her demand lacked conviction.

Blue eyes glinting, Mac laughed deep in his throat. 'You think I'm controlling? Sweetheart, I'll *show* you controlling!'

'This is a game, baby, just a game. You can free yourself any time you want to…see?' With deft movements Mac demonstrated how easy it was to loosen the silk scarves he'd tied her wrists to the bedpost with. Eyes wide, almost luminous, Tara nodded. Her whole body burned for him and he was being deliberately slow, languid, taunting her with sizzling little glances from beneath those outrageous golden lashes of his. He'd stripped off his T-shirt and the sight of that muscular, lean torso with his powerful shoulders and slightly bulging biceps made her clench her thighs in hungry anticipation. Already she was damp for him, more than ready. But tonight Mac's seduction wasn't going to be hard and fast. Tonight he was purposefully taking his time, drawing out the tension between them with every velvet stroke of his fingers, every hot touch of his mouth against her heated flesh. Sliding her dress up to her thighs, he eased down the silky black scrap of underwear along with her tights and discarded them. Then, as Tara strove to keep her legs together, he coaxed them apart with sensuous little nips of his teeth up the inside of her thigh. Finally, when she relaxed, he opened her with his finger, sliding in and out of her wetness as she writhed on the bed and tugged on her binds as if to free herself. But she didn't want to be free. Right now she wanted this slow, sweet torment more than she wanted her next breath. Gasping with pleasure, she felt herself dissolve when Mac positioned himself right between her legs and kissed her intimately. The ceiling spun, her head throbbed and the blood in her veins simmered with scorching heat. The air around them grew cloying and damp, musky with the scent of desire. Tara cried out his name when the tension reached fever pitch and finally spilt over in a heated rush all through her body. Convulsing, she felt herself grow limp, her skin moist and her heart beating like some wild bird's suddenly rescued from captivity.

Inexplicably her eyes filled with tears. As they spilled hotly onto her cheeks, Mac was immediately at her side. Reaching up to untie the scarves that held her willing prisoner, he gathered her urgently into his arms. 'What is it, baby? What's wrong?'

'Oh, Mac,' she cried against his bare shoulder, secretly loving the sensation of clean, smooth, taut flesh, breathing in his deliciously sexy masculine scent until every sense she possessed was filled with it. 'That was wonderful.'

Her words broke down the last barrier Mac had erected in his heart. Blue eyes crinkling, he pushed back her hair from her forehead to gaze tenderly into her face—the face he loved more than any other in the whole wide world. 'I love that I can give you pleasure. I love you, Tara. I don't think I've told you that since I came back. It's the reason I wanted us to try again. As soon as I saw you at the museum it was like turning back the clock. My heart was beating so fast I swear I thought I was having a seizure.'

'I felt the same,' she admitted urgently, joy spilling over at the final confirmation that Mac really did love her; that he hadn't just wanted a reconciliation to make up for past mistakes. 'I never stopped loving you, Mac, not in all the years we were apart. I know I helped to drive you away with my constant complaints about you working all the time. I should have been more understanding but all I knew was that you weren't there when I wanted you to be. In future we'll talk about the things that are important to us both, I promise. Do you know that in all the time we were apart I couldn't even look at another man, let alone contemplate another relationship?'

Her husband heard her passionate statement and knew there were no more recriminations. The slate was well and truly clean. Now they could have the kind of marriage that they'd both dreamed about when they first met and the coming baby would make things just about as perfect as they could get. He would never forget the baby they had lost—Gabriel—but their son hadn't been born in vain because learning of his existence had helped Mac realise that he didn't want to lose Tara ever again. And right now a brighter future than he could possibly have envisaged for himself just a mere month ago was more than possible. Together, he and Tara would make it a reality.

'I can't say I'm not happy about that part. Just the thought of you with someone else...'

'You shouldn't be so jealous. I would never betray you.'

'I know that now. I guess I've always known it, if the truth be told.'

'A little jealousy can be OK but I don't want you to give Raj a hard time when you see him next. He's a good friend and I bullied him into taking me dancing. He spent the whole night utterly miserable because he was worried about what you might say if you found out.'

'Then as long as I know he was miserable I can probably afford to be magnanimous towards him.' Grinning, Mac pinched Tara's cheek affectionately.

'Anyway,' she dropped an experimental little kiss on his shoulder, eyeing him teasingly beneath her lashes, 'I think we seriously need to take another look at those "ground rules" of yours and this time *I'm* going to have some input.'

'Never let it be said I'm not open to compromise.'

'Can't prove it by me.'

'So...we really are "home", Mrs Simmonsen?' Mac was easing up the duvet around them both as he spoke. 'Which is wonderful because we do have some unfinished business we need to take care of.'

Her eyes widening, Tara sucked in an anticipatory breath. 'We do?'

Manoeuvring her onto her back, her silky blonde hair spread out behind her on the plump satin pillow, Mac helped her out of her dress then boldly cupped her naked breast. 'We do, sweetheart, and that's a fact.'

EPILOGUE

FLINGING open the twin doors to the boardroom, Mitch Williams did a quick scan of the faces seated round the long, polished table before bringing his gaze attentively to the immaculately dressed man positioned at its head doing the presentation.

'What is it, Mitch?' Knowing it had to be something pretty important for his chief colleague to interrupt a meeting with a potentially very lucrative client and his staff, Mac slipped his hand into his jacket pocket to check his mobile phone was in reach. He would never normally leave it switched on during a meeting but, circumstances being what they were, he wasn't taking any chances.

'It's Tara,' was all Mitch got out before Mac strode the length of the boardroom to reach his side, his handsome face sharp with concern.

'What's happened?' Blood roared in his ears and he cursed himself for listening to his wife's admonishments of the morning, when she had all but ordered him to go to work because she couldn't stand his prowling round the house like a cat on a hot tin roof. She would be perfectly fine, she'd assured him, and he mustn't worry because the baby wasn't due for at least another week yet. And anyway she'd be spending the day with Beth in the shop, so she'd have help if she needed it.

'She's in Reception. Said she's been having some

niggling pains.' Frowning, Mitch almost looked as if *he* was the anxious father-to-be and not Mac.

'Reception?' Mac echoed loudly and every face in the room turned interestedly towards him. 'What the hell is she doing in Reception?'

She was helping herself to some water from the cooler, a flotilla of shopping bags at her feet—which incidentally were bare because she'd characteristically kicked off her shoes—and she actually smiled at Mac as he hurried towards her into the swish reception area, as if it were the most natural thing in the world for her to be there. 'I'm sorry I interrupted your meeting but I'm afraid I was taken by surprise when I was out shopping.'

Mac shook his head as if to make sure he had all his faculties about him. He was having trouble grasping the fact that his heavily pregnant wife had apparently decided to travel up to London on a shopping spree when she was going to give birth any day now.

'Are you all right? What the hell are you playing at, Tara? You're meant to be at home, resting. Good God, woman! When are you ever going to do what's best for you?'

His words seemed to roll over her like water over the proverbial duck's back. Shrugging casually, she took a sip of her drink before answering. 'I suddenly felt restless. I just had to get out of the house.'

'You were supposed to be going to Beth's. Does she know you came up to London alone?'

'Don't blame Beth for this. Peter asked her to lunch and I said of course she must go. Anyway, rather than wait for her to come back I thought I'd pop on the train and come to London. I got some lovely things for the baby but then I—' Her pretty face contorting suddenly, she doubled over, clutching her very pregnant stomach beneath the floaty summer dress she wore. Mac's heart nearly jumped straight out of his chest. Rushing to her side, he slipped one arm behind her to give support and brushed her hair out of her eyes with the other.

'Tara! Tell me what's wrong! For God's sake, talk to me!'

'I think the baby's coming.'

'What?'

'I said I think the baby's...coming. Phew!' Recovering herself, she straightened, unbelievably regarding Mac with a happy little smile playing around her lips. Bereft of words, her husband stared at her as if he'd been poleaxed.

'Don't panic. My contractions are about twenty minutes apart so we have some time to spare before things really start happening.'

Hardly registering the humour in her voice, Mac swung round to the attractive redhead on the reception desk. 'Astrid, get on the telephone to the emergency services. I want an ambul—'

'Can't we take your car?' Tara interrupted. 'I'm booked into the Portland, which is only five minutes up the road—hardly worth bothering the ambulance people for.'

'You're crazy, you know that?' Cupping her face between his hands, Mac stared into her laughing green eyes and thought, if God blessed him with a hundred lifetimes with this woman, he would never get enough of her.

'You think this is crazy?' she teased back. 'Wait till you see me in a couple of hours' time, screaming my head off and verbally ripping you to shreds.'

*   *   *

At nine o'clock on a balmy summer's evening at the end of June, Tara and Mac Simmonsen became the proud parents of a beautiful baby girl. They called her Brigid after the Irish saint who was associated with healing, poetry and learning because already they had high aspirations for their child. Brigid's mother said she would probably grow up to be a prima ballerina because her legs were long and she already had an imperious air about her which spoke of great things to come, while her father—her father just took one look at her sublime infant perfection and knew he had met the second female in his life who would keep his heart captive. Whatever she did, whatever she became, as long as she was happy it would be all right with him.

HARLEQUIN Presents®

UNCUT

Even more passion for your reading pleasure...

Escape into a world of intense passion and scorching romance! You'll find the drama, the emotion, the international settings and happy endings that you've always loved in Harlequin Presents. But we've turned up the thermostat just a little, so that the relationships really sizzle.... Careful, they're almost too hot to handle!

This September, in

TAKEN FOR HIS PLEASURE
by Carol Marinelli
(#2566)...

Sasha ran out on millionaire Gabriel Cabrini— and he has never forgiven her. Now he wants revenge.... But Sasha is determined not to surrender again, no matter how persuasive he may be....

Also look for MASTER OF PLEASURE (#2571) by bestselling author Penny Jordan. Coming in October!

She's in his bedroom,
but he can't buy her love....

Showered with diamonds,
draped in exquisite lingerie,
whisked around the world...

The ultimate fantasy becomes a reality
in Harlequin Presents!

When Nora Lang acquires some business
information that top tycoon Blake Macleod
can't risk being leaked, he must keep Nora
in his sight.... He'll make love to her for
the whole weekend!

MISTRESS FOR A WEEKEND
by Susan Napier

Book #2569,
on sale September 2006